THE ART OF BEING REMMY

Written and illustrated by Mary Zisk

A blast from the past—with hopes for the future

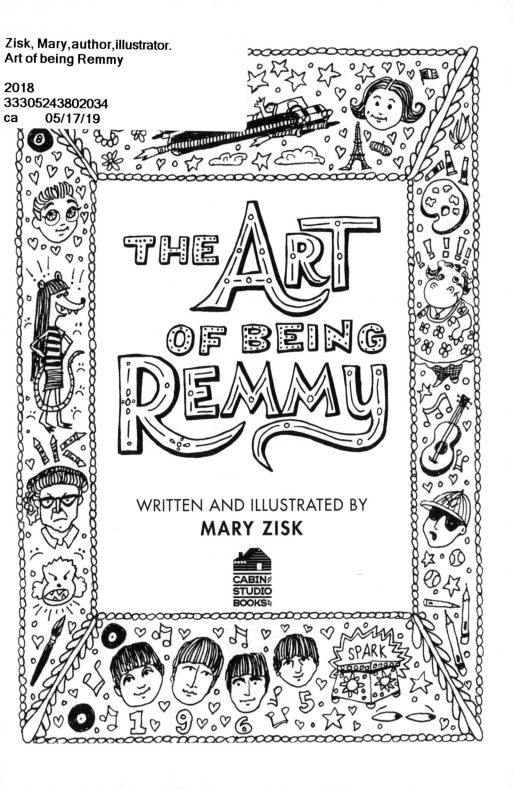

THE ART OF BEING REMMY

WRITTEN AND ILLUSTRATED BY
MARY ZISK

CABIN
STUDIO
BOOKS

ISBN 978-1-7324877-0-3 (case bound hard cover)

Summary: In this funny, illustrated, coming-of-age novel, when mid-1960s attitudes kept girls in their place, 12-year-old Remmy Rinaldi is determined to be an artist, in spite of her father's objections, competition from a boy, and possibly losing her best friend.

BISAC Categories:
JUV003000 JUVENILE FICTION / Art & Architecture
JUV039140 JUVENILE FICTION / Social Themes / Self-Esteem & Self-Reliance
JUV039060 JUVENILE FICTION / Social Themes / Friendship
JUV014000 JUVENILE FICTION / Girls & Women
JUV016150 JUVENILE FICTION / Historical / United States / 20th Century
JUV013060 JUVENILE FICTION / Family / Parents

CABIN
STUDIO
BOOKS

Printed in the United States of America

For all art teachers,
and mine in particular—
Mrs. Henckler, Mr. Weil, and Mr. Becker.

That Was Then...

"My, my," Miss Krasner said and broke into a wide smile. Our art teacher hovered so close to my desk I could smell her lily-of-the-valley perfume. Her shiny red finger nails shuffled through my artwork.

"You really are a regular little Rembrandt, aren't you?"

Rembrandt? The famous artist? My heart exploded.

The eyes of all my third-grade classmates were on me. A couple of kids snickered, but my then-pal Bill Appleton grinned. He understood what I was feeling.

My best friend Debbie, on the other hand, was so engrossed in drawing curlicue hearts around the name "Elvis" on a pink piece of paper with a magenta crayon that even if the real Elvis shimmied into the room right now, she wouldn't notice.

Patting me on the shoulder, Miss Krasner leaned down and whispered, "I think you have the spark of an artist, Rosella. Don't ever lose it."

The Spark of an Artist! No way I'd lose it.

I just didn't know then that I'd have to fight for it.

1

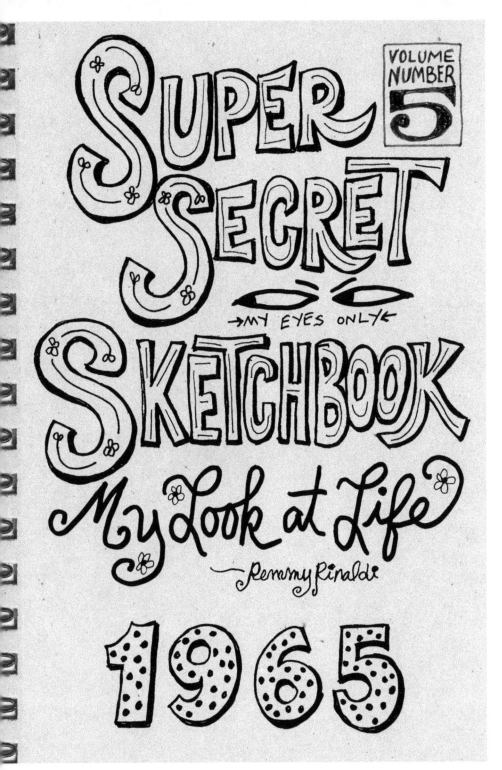

1 • ... And This Is Now

Debbie and I stride into Benjamin Franklin Junior High this first day after Christmas vacation, heads held high, each confident in our New Year's resolutions and ready to start 1965 with a bang.

As we turn a corner, BAM! Bill Appleton belches in my face with the force of an atomic bomb.

"Gaaa!!" I jump back, frantically wave my hand through the air to get rid of his banana-fumed breath, and trip into Debbie who yelps and pushes me off quickly to check her shiny shoes for scuffs.

My dopey enemy Bill has struck in just the first few seconds of school! I glare daggers at his back as he continues down the hall with a laughing herd of goofball boys.

"Good one, Bill!" says one of them as they all laugh and shake Bill's shoulder and pat his crew cut head.

Holy buzz cut! You'd think he just struck out a baseball player on a 3-2 count the way they're congratulating him.

Debbie just whispers "gross" when the boys are out of earshot.

"Yeah, gross. The grossest. Nothing's worse than a smart-aleck seventh-grade knucklehead boy," I say. Yuck, the banana smell is stuck in my nostrils.

"Fortunately not all boys are knuckleheads." Debbie has recovered from our collision. She brushes off her skirt, raises her chin, and touches her hair to check her flip. "Obviously, I go for more sophisticated boys. You know, like Jacques."

Obviously.

I nod in agreement, trying to be supportive of my best friend's optimistic New Year's resolution. She's totally obsessed with this new kid Jacques just because he's French. I told her he's not really French and that he's only French-Canadian which isn't the same, but she's determined that he'll be her boyfriend.

Aside from the French thing, I really don't get the attraction. He's a skinny kid with black horn-rimmed glasses, a strange swoopy haircut held together with greasy Brylcreem, and wears weird clothes like cardigans and straight slacks. Totally not my dream type. But sadly, no seventh-grade boy at Benjamin Franklin Junior High looks anything like a dreamy Beatle. Not even close.

My New Year's resolution has nothing to do with a boy. Ever since my promise to Miss Krasner (and to myself), I've done all I can to keep My Spark burning.

The crummy thing is that I've had to keep my Spark a secret from Dad because he had a cow when I told him and Mom what Miss Krasner said.

"No daughter of mine will ever become an artist, so help me God," Dad growled in his King-of-the-Castle voice. And God must be the only one who knows why Dad feels this way because Dad won't explain and God hasn't let me in on the secret.

But I *am* an artist. So I just kept making art and hid it from Dad in my Super Secret Sketchbook since third grade. Mom has silently disagreed with Dad all these years and believes in my talent so much that she gives me a new sketchbook as soon as I fill up the old one. I'm already up to Super Secret Sketchbook: Volume Number 5.

My first year of junior high should be all about growing into the person I truly am. It's time for me to follow my dream out in the open and become the great artist I know I can be. No more hiding.

That's my New Year's resolution.

1965 is The Year of My Spark. Whether Dad likes it or not.

"Remmy, would you hold my binder for a sec?"

I gladly help while Debbie rummages through her pocketbook.

Kids have called me Remmy ever since Miss Krasner proclaimed I was a regular little Rembrandt. It's a nickname I can actually live up to and it's tons better than being called "Ro-smella" by mean kids.

Debbie continues her rummaging, and I notice she sort of glows today—not just from the tips of her polished penny loafers to her red and green plaid jumper to her perfect flip hairdo, but somehow even from the inside out, like her optimistic resolution has taken over her soul and she radiates.

Maybe Debbie does have a chance of reeling in Jacques. After all, she's pretty, like that movie star Sandra Dee, except she's brunette instead of blond, and a little plump instead of movie-star skinny. She has one cute dimple in her left cheek, and a smile as bright and shiny as Broadway lights. She can speak some French, so she's smart, and she loves her cat, so she is compassionate. Yes, Debbie is the whole package.

Even though this is officially The Year of My Spark and I'm glowing with determination on the inside, I'm sure not glowing on the outside. The Tonette perm my mother gave me back in September is growing out so the top of my hair is straight again but the sides spring out like Slinkys.

And who can glow wearing these Christmas presents—a beige v-neck sweater over a white blouse, a brown tweed skirt, white knee socks, brown lace-up shoes, and a brown purse? Santa must be color blind or has been spending way too much time hanging out with those brown reindeer. I look about as glowy as an old wooden telephone pole, and if I'm not careful, I may get covered in pigeons and poop.

At least the milky-white opal hanging from my necklace glows with shimmery flashes of turquoise and chartreuse and magenta like a rainbow fire—all with the sparkle of my resolution.

9

"Always remember your Spark," Mom had whispered when she fastened the special twelfth-birthday gift around my neck.

Debbie finally whips out a ChapStick from her pocketbook and swoops it across her lips just as the class bell sounds and echoes down the tile walls of the hallway.

"Ooh, we're late for homeroom. Later, alligator!" Debbie takes back her binder and marches off, her flip bobbing and pocketbook swinging from her arm. As she walks away from me, I see how her baby fat is rearranging itself into round curves.

Yes, this is junior high and we are changing. But it looks like Debbie has a big head start on me.

2 • My Yummiest Class

After homeroom, I battle and bounce my way through the noisy jungle of kids until I reach the art room. The room is so yummy to me it feels like a candy store with shelves and drawers and cubbies filled with construction paper, newsprint paper, sketching paper, watercolor paper, colored pencils, ebony pencils, pastel pencils, clay, chalk, charcoal, craypas, tempera paint, watercolor paint, magic markers, round brushes, flat brushes, fan brushes, and erasers. I want to sample all of it so much that my teeth hurt.

I walk into the classroom ready to bite into the sweet taste of creativity. Instead, I almost trip over Bill the Belcher sitting right near the door.

"Boo!" He laughs and I dash to the other side of the room and sit as far away from his grossness as I can get. The desks have been set up in a circle like a wagon train waiting for an attack, so I end up having to face my enemy. But at least at this maximum distance, another belch attack can't reach me. I'm safe.

Mr. Neel, the art teacher, lopes around the room handing out large sheets of newsprint paper and ebony pencils to each of us for our lesson. "Welcome back, everyone."

He's tall and lanky and looks like he slept in his rumpled suit that smells of cigarettes. A black and turquoise polka-dot tie dangles loose around his neck. His hair juts out in all different directions like he's constantly having creative brain storms. Where Miss Krasner was bohemian and bubbly, Mr. Neel is kind of disheveled but in a magnetic artsy way.

Across the room, Bill lets out a peal of laughter as he talks to... Jacques? Wow. Yes, that Jacques. Oh, there's no way I'm telling Debbie he's in my class now, or she'll drag me into some dramatic scheme to trap her amour. Sure I'm all for love, but I'd rather be a distant observer than an unwilling accomplice.

Suddenly, as if Bill hears my thoughts through some kind of evil mental telepathy, he looks right at me with piercing, cold eyes.

I quickly look away and fuss with my paper and pencil, pretending to be busy. My pencil rolls off my desk onto the floor and I lunge to get it and—clunk, ouch, oof—my head hits another head as my hand grabs another hand.

Straightening back up, I look into the biggest, most beautiful eyes in the entire world, if not the whole universe.

I gasp.

What is that color? Something between blue and gray, with

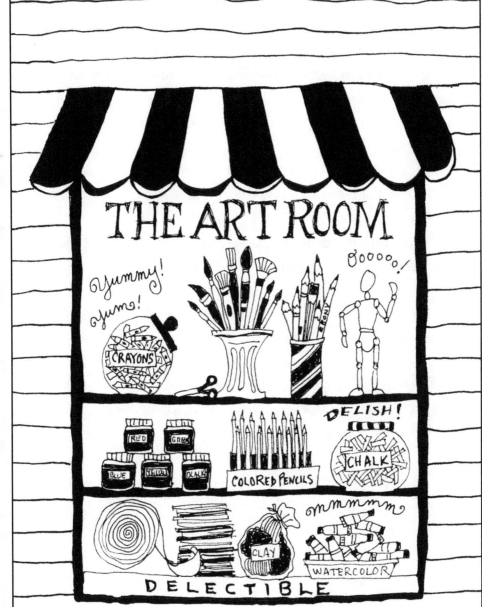

shimmery flecks of green and gold. Some might call it hazel, but that isn't even a special enough word. Like someone would actually have to invent a whole new word to describe the color of those eyes, like "haceliscious" or "blueteousgreen." I think of those sparkling blue-green reflections in Monet's water lily paintings.

My mouth drops open. I'm hypnotized.

Plus, I'm holding hands with Peter McCleary.

"Oops, sorry," says Peter, yanking his hand away and frantically wiping it on his slacks, like he's afraid of getting cooties or something. "I was trying to get your pencil for you. You dropped it."

My hand tingles. The top of my head smarts, but I just keep staring into those haceliscious eyes. They have an adorable Beatle-like quality.

Peter picks up my pencil, hands it to me, and quickly looks down at his paper as the tips of his ears turn bright red.

"Thanks," I whisper.

Why haven't I ever noticed those eyes before? He doesn't wear sunglasses all the time or keep his eyes closed. Maybe I've just never been this close to their power. Suddenly the art room has a whole new magic.

3 • The Year 2000

"Okay, let's get started." Mr. Neel's voice snaps me back to why we are all in this room.

Bill grins at me from across the room, puts his hands on his heart, and makes a kissy face. I stick out my tongue.

"First, I've got an announcement." Mr. Neel runs his fingers through his chaotic hair. "Hopefully you seventh graders have been here at BF long enough to have noticed that large self-portrait on the wall across from the art room. If you haven't, you may not have the observational skills needed to be an artist." He looks seriously stern, but then breaks into a smile.

Of course, I noticed it! I notice everything—diamonds of dew on leaves, the changing color of twilight clouds, yellow snow in the shape of Florida.

The portrait on the wall is larger than life and set into a fancy gold frame. It's so beautiful. The painting, not the frame. And not the man. Actually the man is pretty handsome, too, in an old-fashion Rhett Butler kind of way.

"The artist was Anthony Van Emburgh," Mr. Neel says. "He was born in our town in 1837, attended the Art Students League in New York City, and went on to study in the art capitals of Europe."

Europe. Michelangelo's Rome. Rembrandt's Amsterdam. Vincent van Gogh's Provence. Remmy's *New Jersey*? Not really the same. But imagine all those art treasures in museums and cathedrals and palaces across the Atlantic. I swear I'll see them all some day.

"When Mr. Van Emburgh returned here, he had a very successful career painting portraits of prominent New Jersey residents," Mr. Neel continues.

I've never heard "prominent" and "New Jersey" in the same sentence.

"Now," he says. "Here's the exciting challenge for all of you. Many years ago, his grandson set up the annual Anthony Van Emburgh Art Awards for this school. At the end of the school year, any student may submit four pieces in a portfolio and the top three winners will get U.S. savings bonds."

I straighten up. Neato! Winning will not only bring me fame, but I can prove myself to Dad and a savings bond will really impress him in the wallet. My resolution is actually going to make things happen this year. Now I know it.

"Sorry, Jacques, mon amie, but I'm a cinch to win," I hear Bill

16

snicker. There isn't much of a reaction out of Jacques. He acts more like a tugboat stuck in dry dock instead of the high-powered dreamboat Debbie always babbles about.

But the rest of the classroom buzzes with the thought of winning money, so Mr. Neel claps his hands and speaks louder. "PLUS, I'm adding a new project to this year's contest, just to make things a bit more interesting!"

I slide my eyes sideways to sneak a peek at dreamy Peter, but my eyeballs can't stretch far enough to see his eyeballs. Still, I feel his presence and a tingle in the hand he held.

"How many of you visited the New York World's Fair last summer?" asks Mr. Neel.

Most hands shoot up, but not mine. Dad refused to go because "the gas, the tolls, the parking, and the admission are all too expensive, not to mention any food would be overpriced." Why can't he see beyond money and understand that the World's Fair is a once-in-a-lifetime event? Isn't it worth the cost of the gas, the tolls, the parking, and the admission to visit the whole big world gathered together in Queens? I could skip eating there if that would help.

"Well, the Fair will be re-opening again this spring," Mr. Neel continues. "So it will be your last chance to visit. Some countries are exhibiting their greatest art treasures—like Michelangelo's remarkable marble statue, the *Pieta*, from the Vatican, and works by El Greco, Miro, and Picasso from Spain."

I want to see it all so badly, but using art to convince Dad to go to the Fair would be as impossible as convincing Debbie to drop

17

her dreamboat. Of course Bill's bragging to Jacques about going to the Fair five times already last summer.

"Plus the technology exhibits from America's most visionary companies are mind-boggling!" Mr. Neel is so excited his hair is practically cheering. "There's actually a phone that lets you see the person you're talking to, a futuristic model of underwater cities, and a cool new sports car called a Mustang."

Okay. Our minds are boggled.

"If any of you boys are planning to be astronauts, you can look inside the Mercury space capsule that orbited the Earth, and see a life-size model of the Apollo capsule what will one day fly to the Moon. As our late President Kennedy said, 'We choose to go to the Moon.'" Mr. Neel flings his arms into the air and looks to the heavens. "We've entered the Space Age, and the sky is no longer the limit!" He chuckles at his own wit, but the rest of the room is silent.

"Ahem. Anyway," he says, hiding his hands in his pockets, "in honor of the Fair, I challenge you to create an additional piece of art about the future. Your Vision of the Year 2000. What do you think life will be like 35 years into the future?"

The year 2000? I do some quick math in my head. I'll be ancient by then. 47!

"You know, these days we wonder how can the world get any more modern than it already is. But just think about it." Mr. Neel scratches his head. "Going back in time 35 years ago to 1930, many movies were still silent and all were filmed in black and white. There was no TV, no transistor radios, no jet planes or helicopters,

18

no Frisbees, no sliced bread. Not even a ballpoint pen. Look how far we've come since then."

I love my turquoise transistor radio. I can listen to music anywhere. How could anyone in the future create a better invention than that?

Mr. Neel scans our faces. "Now, going forward in time, think about what kind of progress can happen by the year 2000. Let's see what amazing future world you can imagine."

It all seems so far away. For sure I'll be making art in the year 2000, but what will rest of the world be like? Maybe I'll have a robot maid like the Jetsons so I can make art without being bothered by housework.

"This is so cool! I can think of all kinds of futuristic things! Can't you?"

Peter is talking to me (to ME!) and I'm pulled back into his optical trance.

"Oh, absolutely! Real cool." I sigh. Hazeliscious!

Those eyes will still mesmerize in 35 years.

4 • The Challenge

The bell rings at the end of class, and everyone, including Peter, pours out into the hallway, racing to their next class. But I linger at the self-portrait of Mr. Van Emburgh, observing as much as possible.

His painting technique is so awesome. It's realistic, but also very expressive with lively brush strokes. The skin tones are ruddy pink against greenish shadows and white highlights, his wavy black hair and beard glisten with strands of silver, his maroon velvet jacket looks soft enough to touch, and his steel blue eyes look right at me. I can tell those eyes have seen tons of masterpieces in Europe. He stands tall and looks so confident posing at his easel. He had definitely followed his Spark and was proud of it.

I stretch my spine up, push my shoulders back, and stand tall too.

"Hey, Miss Rembrandt."

I cringe and turn. There is only one bozo who calls me that instead of Remmy.

"So are you entering the Art Awards?" Bill appears at my side, rubbing the stiff top of his crew cut.

"Yeah." I go back to staring into the painter's eyes, hoping Bill will get the hint and scram.

"You don't sound very sure." Bill snorts and then says, "What do you think of Mr. Tony here?"

"I love this portrait." I really do.

I reluctantly look back at Bill. Is that the little twinkle in his eyes he used to get when we worked together on art projects in elementary school? The twinkle I liked. When we had fun and laughed. When we were actually pals.

Bill dramatically sweeps his arm in front of the portrait and says in a booming voice, "Notice that Mr. Tony was a man. You know, all great artists are men."

So that wasn't a twinkle after all. That was pure premeditated nastiness. I break eye contact and start to leave, too angry to challenge his stupid statement.

"Hey, wait!"

I don't know why I stop, but I do.

Bill smirks and continues, "Come on, think about it. Leonardo, Michelangelo, Rubens, Degas, and, of course, my idol, Picasso. All men."

I quickly try to think of a lady artist so I can shoot down his idiotic theory.

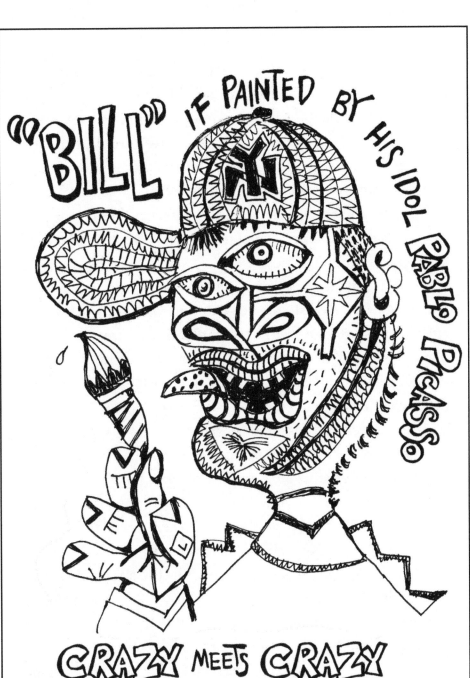

My cousin Vinnie Junior had given me his *History of Art* book from his college class, and when I poured through that fat book page by page by page, there were no lady artists in it at all! In 572 pages! And I went through it three times. Frontwards and backwards. There were plenty of paintings of ladies—a lot of them without clothes on—but no paintings by ladies. None. Zero!

There just have to be lady artists as great as those men.

Aha! I know. I remember an artist on the cover Life magazine. "What about Grandma Moses?"

"Ha! If you want to call those cutesy country scenes art. She's only famous because she started painting when she was already elderly and lived to be over 100 years old. You can't even compare her to the incredible Pablo Picasso! He started painting when he was only seven." Bill laughs. "There's such power and excitement in his work. Boy, would I love to shake Picasso's hand!"

"Isn't he dead?" I ask innocently.

Bill glares at me as if I had just tried to kill off his idol. "Are you kidding? He's still going strong. He's like a bull."

Yeah. Bull.

Except Bill actually may be right. Where are all the women artists? Just me and Grandma Moses?

"Speaking of great art, you should see the oil paintings I've been doing at Mrs. Egan's studio." Bill crows like some hot-shot rooster, practically flapping his wings. "With those paintings, I'm a shoe-in to win Mr. Tony's Art Award. First place, of course."

"You're painting in oils?" Curses! Bill really could clobber me in the contest with that kind of training. I had heard that a mom in the neighborhood is giving kids painting lessons.

"Why even bother entering, Miss Rembrandt? There's no chance you can beat me." Bill doesn't wait for my reaction and struts away down the hall, laughing.

That dumb arrogant knucklehead!

It's The Year of My Spark!

Of course I can beat him!

Probably.

Maybe.

Mr. Tony looks down at me sympathetically. I look back. I touch my opal and know I have to do everything I can to take those painting lessons, too.

Then when I win the award, Bill won't be laughing.

Yeah, he'll see.

When I win.

If I win.

5 • The Plea Over Pot Roast

Dad scoops up the last of the mashed potatoes on his plate and they disappear into his mouth. While he cuts a piece of pot roast, Mom grabs the empty potato bowl off the table, scurries into the kitchen, returns with the bowl refilled and steamy, and hands it to Dad. They exchange a smile.

The only noise in the dining room is the clinking of forks and knives on plates. I push around some peas until they form a frown. I sneak a peek at my father, but he's engrossed in his pot roast.

I'm going to ask Dad to let me take painting lessons. Debbie made me pinky-swear that I would. She said if she had the courage to pursue Jacques, then I should be brave enough to ask Dad. We have a duty to stick to our New Year's resolutions. Her French Dreamboat. My Spark of an Artist. No backing out.

So, I'm going to ask.

Yes.

I am.

Soon.

I look past Mom to her shrine on the dining room wall. The framed portraits of the Three Heavenly Catholics—Jesus, Good Pope John XXIII, and President Kennedy—look back at me.

All my relatives have these three hanging somewhere in their houses. Jesus used to be in Mom and Dad's bedroom and Good Pope John XXIII hung in my grandma Nonna's room. Then, when poor handsome President Kennedy was assassinated more than a year ago, Mom moved his portrait out of the kitchen and gathered all Three Heavenly Catholics together in the dining room.

Whenever I pass them, their eyes follow me and make me feel guilty, even when I haven't done anything wrong. But tonight, I honestly feel like they are all on my side. They want me to ask.

"Okay."

Dad stops in mid-chew.

Did I say that out loud?

"Okay what?" Mom asks.

The Three Heavenly Catholics look impatient so I take a deep breath and keep talking.

"Um, I found out today that there is an art contest at school and the winner gets a savings bond and I really think I can win, but Bill is taking painting lessons with Mrs. Egan, and I need to take them too so I can beat him because he says girls can't be great artists and..."

27

Dad gives me his ominous look that reminds me of the painting of Henry XIII by Holbein—as if Dad's about to shout, "Off with her head!"

"NO! Absolutely not. No painting lessons." Dad's eyebrows twitch. "We've talked about this in the past and you know any further discussion is pointless. You will NOT be an artist!"

I look at Mom for support. She gives me a half-smile, and looks back at her plate.

I telepathically send a quick prayer to the Three Heavenly Catholics. Please make Dad see me for the true artist I am, and make him brush the cobwebs off his wallet, and pay for the lessons.

My hand moves to my opal to give me courage and I sit up straight. "But, Dad, it's really not that much money."

"Ro-sel-la Ma-ri-a Ri-nal-di!"

I slump in my chair. Whenever Dad says every single syllable of my name like a clacking typewriter, I know I'm in trouble. Big trouble.

"This is not about money," Dad says. "Although, besides the cost of lessons, there's the paints, the canvases, the brushes. It all adds up." He holds out his thumb and adds digits as he continues. "That could cost at least $25, maybe even $30! Cripes! That's as much as that modern five-speed blender your mother's been begging for."

Mom nods her head but won't look at me.

I thought this wasn't about money.

"Well, it's a moot point because the last thing I would ever use my hard-earned money for is art supplies."

Oh no. Here it comes.

The Great Depression Speech.

"You kids these days don't know what it's like to be poor," Dad says. "I grew up in New York City tenements during the Great Depression. I know what it's like to be without money."

Yep, The Speech. And here comes The Joke.

"Money back then was tighter than your Aunt Teresa's girdle."

I mouth the words along with Dad as he says them.

"Teresa loves her spaghetti! Ha ha ha!"

Dad always cracks himself up with this lame joke. But according to Nonna, those tough times were no laughing matter. The stock market crashed, millions of people lost money and jobs and homes. But that was over thirty years ago.

"Other kids are taking Mrs. Egan's class and I'm just as good as they are. Maybe better." I don't even know if this is true, so I apologize to the Three Heavenly Catholics with my eyes. "It's critical that I learn to paint. Real artists paint!"

"Critical? So you think this is a life-or-death situation? To be a real artist?" He shakes his head.

I take a deep breath. "Well, I went to see Mrs. Egan and she says..."

"That Peggy Egan is a kook." Dad rolls his eyes. "Look at those crazy getups she wears. And out in public. How can her husband allow her to parade around like that?"

"She's not a kook," I say.

"Well, sweetie," Mom says to me just above a whisper, "you

have to admit her wardrobe is somewhat inappropriate. So bohemian." She plays with the strand of pearls around her neck.

"Mrs. Egan looks neato. And she thinks I'm an artist. And that's what I'm going to be!" She saw my talent when I showed her my Super Secret Sketchbook.

Dad leans forward. "No beatnik, artsy housewife is going to tell me what's best for my own daughter!" His eyes soften a little and the volume of his voice drops. "Rosella, you can't imagine the kinds of struggle, the sacrifices, and pain an artist faces. Believe me. People get hurt. I've seen it. You will NOT be an artist!"

Jesus, the Pope, and JFK look dismayed. Maybe they're as confused as I am about Dad.

"So what are we having for dessert, dear?" That's Dad Code for: Case closed, new topic.

My napkin is twisted into a tight knot. I place it on the table. "I'd like to be excused, please."

"But I've baked your favorite, sweetie. Pineapple upside-down cake." Mom starts to stand. "I'll go get it."

"No, thank you." I race out of the dining room.

6 • Where's the Money?

I can't get to my bedroom fast enough, taking two stairs at a time. I slam the door, crank up my transistor radio as loud as it goes. As if the radio reads my mind, Lesley Gore comes on and belts out "You Don't Own Me."

"...and don't tell me what to do..." I sing along through my tears. Lesley's singing to a boyfriend, but her song applies to dads, too. At least to mine it does.

Dad has always made it very clear that he won't let me be an artist, but he hasn't made it clear why. That's the big mystery. What happened? Did an artist smack him on the head with a palette? Did an artist cheat him out of money? Did an artist paint an insulting portrait of him?

My eyes are puffy and heavy from crying. I curl up under my afghan and hug my pillow for comfort. I squeeze my eyes closed and try to block out the hurt. I can't help that I was born an artist. I can't just bury it deep inside of me. My brain can't deal with this and I drift off to sleep.

I'm floating and reeling through a night sky that looks like an ocean filled with waves and swirls of every possible color of blue. The sky whirls over a village and holds rings of yellow stars and the Moon. A dark tree rises out of the landscape like flames and tries to catch me. But I'm not afraid because I know exactly where I am and I couldn't be happier. I'm swimming through Vincent van Gogh's painting, The Starry Night.

I roll around the bold brush strokes and swim through the motion of the sky, around the bright stars. The Moon turns into a milky-white opal shimmering with flashes of turquoise and chartreuse and magenta. My Spark. I stretch out to touch it but it drifts out of reach. I try to pull myself through the blue waves of sky but the opal Moon slides farther and farther away from me. I can't catch it. But this is the year I must.

I wake up to a brightness shining in my eyes. The full moon is outside my window spilling a stripe of light across me and my bed. The rest of my bedroom is dark.

I flick on my bedside lamp and see that it is 1:30 in the morning. My transistor radio is silent and there is a piece of pineapple upside down cake on my desk. Mom has been here. I'm not hungry.

My dream is still fresh in my mind as is my determination to

33

Dreamy Floating Through Starry Night

follow my Spark. Neither will fade. I must take those lessons.

Across my room is the one place in the world that not only stirs up my creative juices, but comforts me at the same time—my floor-to-ceiling bedroom wall covered with corkboard. My WOW!WALL.

When anyone comes into my room, they freeze, look at the Wall, and say "WOW!" Wow can either mean, "Wow, that's so cool" or "Wow, that's scary." I've gotten pretty good at looking at their eyes and telling which Wow means what.

Dad's never even seen it since he never comes in my room—like there's some threatening girly force field that would burn out his eyes.

But Mom has seen it. She made the WOW!WALL possible. When Dad was out of town for a conference, she and I went to Woolworth's and bought peel-and-stick cork tiles and got to work. Wow!

Every artist needs inspiration and visual stimulation, so anything that makes my eyes happy and makes me think WOW! gets put on the Wall—prints of my favorite paintings, etchings, and drawings, photos of cute TV and movie stars, pages from magazines, postcards and souvenirs, baseball cards, Sunday comics, and Beatles, Beatles, Beatles (Debbie's fave section of the Wall)! It's like the world's most humungous scrapbook. This is the place that tickles my eyes and sets off firecrackers of creativity in my mind.

As my eyes settle on the bold brushstrokes in a postcard of *The Starry Night*, I'm more and more convinced by my dream that

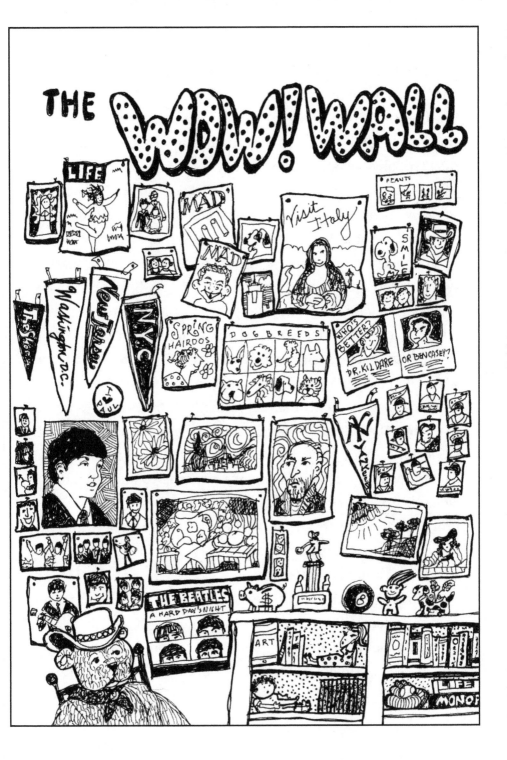

learning to paint in oils is going to push my talents up to a new level. If there's any chance of me winning the Art Awards and beating Bill, I have to take Mrs. Egan's lessons even if it means sneaking behind Dad's back. But where will I get the money?

The obvious starting point is my piggy bank, but I'm not optimistic. I pick up Oinker and shake. Not very noisy. Maybe I have so many dollar bills stuffed in the bank that they are muffling the sound of the coins. I pry open Oinker's tummy and quickly see the lack of noise is due to the lack of money. One dollar bill, a quarter, two pennies, a button, and a five-cent stamp. So much for my savings. I shouldn't have bought so many Beatles trading cards with my allowance. Now I have to find a way to actually make money.

Debbie makes really good money babysitting. She's a natural with all those domestic-type skills—wrangling kids, cooking, cleaning, sewing. I only babysat a couple of times and it's fun to play when the kids are awake. But when they go to bed and I'm all alone in the living room, I hear creaks and bumps and rattles and I get the heebie-jeebies. I freeze in front of the TV and listen to the clock tick off the seconds until the parents come home. Well, I pretty much hate babysitting, so scratch that idea. There must be less uncomfortable ways to make money.

What can I do? I need help here.

Barbie lounges in my bookcase and looks totally indifferent to my problem with that permanently-haughty stare in her eyes.

My good luck troll with its chartreuse hair grins at me from the top shelf. I rub its belly for luck, but I need more than that. I need a plan.

Then I see it. Next to my troll.

Yes! Magical help!

I grab my good old shiny black Magic 8 Ball and feel its weight and promise. I shake it hard. C'mon, make some magic.

"Will I find a way to pay for painting lessons?" I ask the Ball.

I flip over the shiny black ball and watch the words slowly come into focus in the window.

"Reply hazy. Try again."

Curses! Not even the Ball believes in me. I shake the Ball and ask my question again. I wait, holding my breath.

"The answer will come," it says.

All right! I breathe out a sigh of relief and belief, and climb back into bed.

The Magic 8 Ball has spoken.

The answer will come.

7 • The Cafeteria Double Ambush

A week later, I'm still waiting for the answer to come. I'm also waiting for Debbie to join me. She is lurking at the busy entrance to the cafeteria—a stealth agent in Operation Jacques. Operation or no Operation, if she takes much longer, I'll forget about being polite and dig into my chicken a la king without her. It's already getting cold and lumpy.

Kids continue to swarm in, grab trays, and get on the lunch line. Through all the commotion, Debbie is totally focused on her mission.

From her post, Debbie checks every face that passes through the doorway. She has stepped up her master plan of pursuit, although so far this week she has had a zero percent success rate. Maybe today will be the day.

Suddenly, Debbie's inner radar locks in on her target and she jumps into action. Debbie zips and zooms through kids until she is directly behind Jacques in the lunch line. Stage One accomplished.

When they reach the lunch ladies, Debbie moves on to Stage Two and motions to different selections, all the while smiling at Jacques and touching his arm. She keeps chattering at him, touching her flip, as they go past the dessert selections. Then she reaches in front of him and places a milk carton on his tray. Jacques stands as stiff as a statue the whole time Debbie is flirting. He quickly pulls coins out of his pocket, throws them at the cashier, and races to the far end of the cafeteria to join Bill's loud gang of goofballs.

Debbie waves at his back, and heads toward me with a happy bounce. She sets her tray down on the table and flashes a big mission-accomplished smile.

"Jacques really appreciated my advice about the food selections. I suggested he take the hot roast beef sandwich and he did! You know what that means, right?"

"He doesn't like chicken a la king?" I ask as I finally dig into mine.

"No! He trusts me. He values my opinion." Debbie cranes her neck in the direction of the goofballs' table where Jacques has successfully hidden himself.

"Did he even talk to you?" I ask.

"Well, sure he did. Kind of. When he took the plate from the lunch lady, he said thanks, which sounded like he was talking to her, but I know he was actually thanking me for my help."

I roll my eyes at her delusion.

"I saw that!" Debbie wags a finger at me. "My plan is totally working. I'm breaking down his barriers of shyness and it won't be long."

"Won't be long until what?" I ask.

Debbie's eyes get a faraway, lovey-dovey look. "Until we're laughing together and sharing secrets and telling each other our truest feelings."

"I don't think boys do that." I really don't.

"Of course they do that. They're human beings!"

"Are you sure?"

"Oh stop. Now you're just mocking me." Debbie pushes out her lower lip in a make-believe pout. Then we both giggle.

Debbie cuts up some of her roast beef sandwich and pokes around at the mashed potatoes. I know she really prefers chicken a la king. Ah, the sacrifices for love.

I jab my fork into a big chunk of chicken swimming in yellow cream sauce and gobble it down. Debbie just watches.

"Well, at least you're following through on your New Year's resolution." I toast her with my milk carton. "I haven't even been able to start."

"But this is the year of your spark." Debbie looks concerned.

"You know my Dad. The only way I can take painting lessons is to..."

"Dominique! Bonjour!" A deep unfamiliar voice interrupts me.

An extremely tall slender girl looms over our table, smiling at Debbie. Long black hair reaches halfway down her back and thick bangs almost cover her beady amber eyes. No one in school looks like this girl, like she's from a different planet or stepped out of a painting by Modigliani.

"Bonjour!" Debbie beams up at this Eiffel Tower of a girl and then notices my puzzled face. "Oh, 'Dominique' is my name in French class. This is Suzanne. Isn't it cool that her name is the same in French and American? She just started school here."

"Hi, I'm Remmy. Welcome to BF, Suzy," I say, swallowing my problem and sending her my best glad-to-meet-you smile.

The Eiffel Tower's eyes give me the once over. "I'm Suzanne."

Then she looks straight at Debbie and says, "Isn't this cafeteria food just dreadful? I brought in some napoleons to share with the class. You'll love them."

"*Naturellement*! They're French." Debbie turns to me. "Rem, Suzanne's actually lived in France! Can you believe it?"

No, I can't believe it. "Wow, have you been to the Louvre? Did you see the Mona Lisa?"

"Of course. How could I not?" She flicks her hair over her shoulder. "I've seen many remarkable things in Europe. My father's in the military so we've moved a lot. France is divine—so sophisticated and stylish." The Eiffel Tower scowls and scans the cafeteria. "Not like *New Jersey*."

This girl is not being very divine. Her voice sounds slithery.

"Then why are you here in *New Jersey*, anyway?" I ask.

The Eiffel Tower rolls her eyes and sighs. "We had to move in with my grandparents because my father was deployed to Vietnam." Her mouth makes a funny crinkled shape like she just

43

bit into a lemon. "He's going to defeat the communists, you know."

"Single-handedly?" I open my eyes wide in fake admiration. If she didn't have such an attitude, I'd be kinder. I'd be a total mess if my dad was fighting in a war and I want to be sympathetic, but she's a pretty unsympathetic creature.

Suzanne ignores my question and quickly turns her attention to Debbie. "Love your outfit, Dominique! *Tres chic!*"

"You were right about wearing blue to bring out my eyes."

Suzanne and Debbie actually squeal.

"Well, got to run, *mon amie.*" Suzanne turns on her heel, her hair flying like a scarf. "See you in French!" and she strides out the door.

That was an unpleasant interruption, although Debbie seemed to enjoy it.

I'm just about to talk to Debbie about my Dad dilemma when a loud thundering of male voices interrupts, shouting words like "foul shot, moron, charging," mixed in with laughter. The herd of goofballs gallops by.

"Hey, isn't that the famous artist Miss Rembrandt?" Bill waves and stays with the herd, saying to the others, "You guys know the Knicks are gonna clobber those Celtics."

I spot Peter (hazeliscious!) nodding at Bill, but he doesn't notice me.

Debbie cranes her neck to get a better view. I see a sliver of Jacques hiding behind Bill as they all rumble out of the cafeteria.

Debbie looks around the emptying cafeteria. "Where did he go?"

"Who?"

Debbie frowns and shakes her head. "Don't you ever stop joking?" She stands and picks up the tray with her uneaten lunch. "I'll see you later. Glad I have Suzanne's *délicieux* dessert to look forward to."

Suzanne.

That girl's up to something.

8 • Digging In

Snow covers all the lawns and makes the neighborhood look so much like a Bruegel snow painting that I expect to see a group of hunters returning from the woods with their hounds.

I trudge up the street, flapping a piece of mail in the air like a fan, and head to the Zabriskie house at the top of the hill.

The house is stone and as old as history, maybe even as old as George Washington. Surrounded by modern split-level houses, it looks as out of place as a grandpa sitting on one of those tiny chairs in a classroom full of kindergartners.

The neighborhood sidewalks are clear of snow until they stop at the edge of the Zabriskie property. I slide out into the slushy street, and carefully walk around the large yard until I find snow-covered steps that lead to the front door.

I trudge up the steps and face a faded, peeling, gray front door.

Not finding a doorbell, I rap the heavy doorknocker. The sound of quick clickety-clackety nails running on a wood floor and then yapping and scratching come from the other side of the door. Next I hear slow shuffling feet and then a piercing, gravelly voice.

"Fluffy! Fluffy! Hush up, you furry old squawk box!"

The lace curtains behind the front door's window part very slightly. A pair of thick glasses with two slits of eyes look at me and then the gravelly voice says, "What do you want?"

"I have a piece of your mail," I shout at the door.

An "ooff" come out of Fluffy, and the door creaks open. The dog wriggles in Mrs. Zabriskie's arms, and shows me his pointy teeth—at least, the few that are left. Fluffy has to be the oldest, nastiest, angriest poodle I've ever seen. Maybe he just hates his sissy name.

Mrs. Zabriskie leans forward and squints through her glasses into my face. "And who might you be?"

"I'm Remmy. I live down at the bottom of the hill. On Meadow Lane."

"Bah! Meadow Lane. That used to be a *real* meadow before all those gall darn modern boxes got built on our land. A meadow with wild flowers and butterflies. Now there's just yard after yard of perfect green lawns. I'll never forgive my Walter for selling off our land." She raises a boney fist at the sky. "You hear me, Walter? Never!"

"We got your mail by mistake." As I hand her the envelope, Fluffy snaps at the air. I'm very ready to get out of here.

"Oh, Merciful Lord, my social security check!" She drops

CHORES TO DO FOR MRS. ZABRISKIE:

(and FLUFFY) →

1. CARRY **LAUNDRY** DOWN TO THE BASEMENT.

2. DUST CERAMIC **CHICKEN COLLECTION** ON TOP OF THE KITCHEN CABINETS.

3...4...5... ETC, ETC, **WHATEVER** COMES UP.

Fluffy to the floor and blocks him with her foot. "I was all discombobulated when this wasn't in yesterday's mail."

I don't like the way Fluffy is eyeing me and back away from the door. "Well, I gotta go."

"Wait." Mrs. Zabriskie's frown breaks into a smile. "I need to thank you. What did you say your name was?"

"Remmy."

"Remmy? That's a name? For gracious sakes! Sounds like a medical condition," Mrs. Zabriskie clucks.

"Well, it's a nickname. My real name is Rosella."

"Rosella?" She gives me an odd look, like I'm an alien. "Is that eye-talian?"

"Yes, Ma'am. Look, I really need to get going..."

"My stars and garters!" she yelps in that piercing voice.

I jump, then freeze. What did I do?

The little lady adjusts her glasses and looks around her yard.

"I don't get out very often and didn't realize how much the snow has piled up. That walkway looks treacherous. You could have been hurt, Rosie!"

"Uh, Remmy."

"Sure." A sad cloud passes over Mrs. Zabriskie's face. "My Walter used to take such good care of our yard. He only passed away early last spring, just before his roses came into full bloom."

"I'm so sorry," I say, still keeping an eye on snarling Fluffy.

"I had that boy Skippy mowing the lawn, but now he's gone off to college. He could have taken care of this snow." Mrs. Zabriskie lets out a chuckle. "Skippy! There's another name.

Imagine, a college man named Skippy!"

She looks from the snow and back to me. "Do you know a strong young man who could shovel snow for me? I would pay him."

"I'm not sure." I bet dreamy, hazeliscious-eyed Peter is strong and might be really happy if I got him a job. No. I'm not brave enough to ask him. Who else?

I sure wouldn't set Bill up with a job since he's been such a jerk. And besides, he's already taking Mrs. Egan's painting class, and I'm the one with the skinflint father who won't pay for lessons.

"OH!" I shout. "That's it!"

Mrs. Zabriskie jumps.

Fluffy yelps.

The Magic 8 Ball was right. The answer has come.

"YES! I can shovel your snow! I'm strong." I can earn money to pay for painting lessons. Who needs Dad?

"Oh, but this is boy's work," says Mrs. Zabriskie, shaking her head. Fluffy growls in agreement.

"Please, please, please. Give me a chance." I try to make my eyes look puppy-dog-irresistible. "Pleeeeeease."

"For pity's sake," she says. "Okay. You've got a job. I'll pay you two dollars."

"It's a deal."

"The shovel is out back in the shed."

I get right to work and slog my way through the snow to the shed way at the back of the property. I find the shovel and make my way back to the house, and shovel down the front steps I had originally trudged up. At the bottom of the steps, there's a cement walkway that's been hidden by the snow, so I shovel that until it takes me to a garage that has a long driveway that curves around back to the street.

I stop and lean on the shovel, breathing hard. Snow has gotten into my boots so my toes are numb and my mittens are soaking wet. I'm exhausted. Maybe Mrs. Zabriskie is right about this being boy's work. But I have to keep going. I need the money. I need to paint.

Finally, after two hours, I finish. I ache so much it feels like I've grown new muscles just to hold the pain. But the two bucks (plus a 25-cent tip) from Mrs. Zabriskie in my pocket act like an instant painkiller.

As I start to leave, Mrs. Zabriskie calls to me.

"You did good, Rosie. I was thinking. Would you be able to come around on Saturdays to help me with chores?"

Fluffy shows me his teeth, letting out a low growl, and I'm about to say no.

"I'll pay you," she yells. "Three dollars every Saturday."

The magic words!

"I'll be back on Saturday and do anything you want!" I wave and head home.

Thank you, Magic 8 Ball!

Yippee! I can build up a painting fund in no time, and before long, I'll be swooshing a brush at Mrs. Egan's. No thanks to Dad.

9 • The Wonder of Woolworth's

After a sweaty class of gymnastics, we all pour into the girls locker room. The locker room smells like old socks and ammonia, and girls' voices bounce around the tiled, steamy room.

"Rem, you want to walk into town after school?" Debbie calls out to me over the room babble.

"Sure. Let's stop at Woolworth's to see if the new *16 Magazine* is in." We always find something to treasure at Woolworth's, especially Beatles stuff.

I cross the room to get to my locker and start unsnapping my ugly gym suit, which is truly the pits—a one-piece maroon blouse and shorts combo. It must have been designed by some vengeful ex-gym teacher to scare boys away from girls who are already plenty worried about what they look like.

I sneak a peek around the room at my classmates and see all

shapes and sizes of bras. I'm still flat as a Necco wafer.

Opening my gym locker, I take my blouse out. I squeeze as close to the locker as possible so that as soon as I get my gym suit off, I can quickly pull my blouse on before the others see my undershirt. I have to be the only girl in seventh grade still wearing baby underwear. Why is my body taking so long to catch up?

I button up my blouse, pull on my green wool jumper, and zip it up. It'd be so liberating to put on my comfy dungarees instead. But it's against school rules—dresses and skirts only for girls— which also seems to be an unwritten rule for grownup ladies. Mom would be mortified being caught in the supermarket in slacks! I just don't get it.

I pull on my knee socks and slide into my loafers.

"Deb, I'll meet you by the office after school," I call as I grab my purse and notebook. I turn to sprint out of the locker room and lock eyes with Suzanne. Her amber eyes flash and she has a smirk on her face. That Eiffel Tower gives me the creeps.

* * * * *

As soon as we walk into Woolworth's, Debbie pulls me over to the photo booth and pushes me in.

"Best friends need new pictures." She squeezes in next to me and puts a quarter into the slot. "SMILE!" A big flash almost blinds me. Laughing, I make a fish face. FLASH. Debbie stretches her mouth with her fingers and sticks out her tongue. FLASH. We squish our heads together, giggling. FLASH.

We tumble out of the booth laughing and wait until the brown and white strip of photos slips out of the slot. I carefully rip the strip in half, two photos for me and two for Debbie.

"These photos will last forever...like our friendship!" I put them safely in my purse.

"That's for sure!" Debbie takes off into the store. "Come on! We need Beatles stuff."

We run down an aisle past coloring books, costume jewelry, and plastic cars. Then up another aisle past parakeets, fish, and turtles. Then down another aisle past dishes, glasses, and girdles. Making one last turn, we finally reach the Beatles display.

"They do have the newest *16 Magazine*! I'm getting it." I read the cover. "'Beatles Wild Wild Bash!' 'Paul's Most Secret Confessions!' Oooh, I've got to read that."

"Let me see!" Debbie grabs the magazine. "Look. 'John King-Size Signed Pin-Up!'"

"I'll give it to you." John Lennon belongs to her and Paul McCartney belongs to me.

"You're the best, Rem," says Debbie.

"Should I also splurge on some Beatles trading cards? I only just started earning money for my painting fund." I already have 35 cards, but I'm still missing some important ones, like #3 and #27.

"I vote for Beatles!"

Of course Debbie would say that. We have a solemn cross-your-heart pledge to see the Beatles in concert together. But I've also pledged to my Spark.

The temptation is too great and I reach for the card packs.

But I'm interrupted by a deep grating noise.

"*Bonjooooourrrrrr!*"

Suzanne suddenly appears like an unwanted pimple.

"If it isn't the Beatlemaniacs." She only looks directly at Debbie. "*Dominique, comment ça va?*"

"*Bien, Suzanne. Qu'est-ce que tu fais?*" Debbie beams at the invading Eiffel Tower.

I nod and pretend to understand their jibberjabber.

"Oh Rem, I forgot to tell you. Suzanne talked me into joining the French Club with her. You know how I adore all things French."

"Especially someone named Jacques!" Suzanne pokes Debbie and they giggle.

"Their fries are okay," I mutter.

"Dominique, come look at the new nail polish colors with me." Suzanne tugs on Debbie's sleeve and then looks down at my hands and chewed finger nails. "You're probably not very interested in nail polish, are you?"

I quickly hide my hands in my pockets and look dagger eyes at this French phony. Debbie's always after me to stop my nail biting, but it's too soothing to give up.

"You know, they sell bras in aisle 7," Suzanne whispers at me. She pulls on Debbie's arm. "Let's go!"

"Rem, I'll only be in the makeup aisle for just a minute." Her eyes look unsure. "Here's a dime. Get me two Beatle card packs, okay?" Debbie hurries after Suzanne and calls back to me, "I'll meet you by the cashier."

While I flip through the *16 Magazine,* I can hear them ooooing and aaaahing in the other aisle. Hmmph, color belongs on canvas, not on fingernails, in my opinion.

A loud cackle coming from the makeup aisle makes me cringe.

I tuck the magazine under my arm. My aggravation makes me grab three packs of Beatle bubblegum cards for myself as a treat. I pick up two packs for Debbie, and pay for everything at the cash register.

I rip open one of the card packs and flip through the cards. Bingo! The Paul #3 card, the one I'm missing! If only Suzanne would hit the road so I can show Debbie my treasure. I also have a double George that she might want to trade for a Ringo.

High-pitched chattering drifts over from the makeup aisle, and I chew my thumbnail. What's taking them so long?

I take out a ballpoint pen and start doodling on the brown paper bag that holds the magazine and cards. First, long dark hair, an evil smile with sharp teeth, then beady eyes, tiny hands with long fingers, and, finally, a long tail. My portrait of Rat Fink Suzanne is complete.

Debbie's laugh and another cackle echo across the store. I look at the duplicate George card I want to trade and sigh. Debbie better not trade me for that Rat Fink.

"Rem!" Debbie waves to me from across the aisles. "We're going to get shakes at the counter. Come on."

I don't want to join them, but I have no choice. Debbie spent entirely too much time alone with Suzanne already and I don't want any more rat-finky cooties contaminating my best friend.

At the lunch counter, I say I'm not thirsty. I need to save every penny for painting lessons, especially after I just splurged on the Beatles cards.

When Suzanne orders a strawberry shake, Debbie does, too. What? Chocolate has always been her favorite.

I distract myself by spinning on the red vinyl counter stool, looking down at the floor to see how long I can spin before I get so dizzy I fall off. Debbie blocks me with her leg and gives me a that-is-so-babyish glare. She turns her attention to the arriving drinks. Boy, I sure am thirsty.

"Do you want a sip?" Debbie holds out her drink to me.

"No thanks. I don't like strawberry." She knows that!

Suzanne takes a big slurp through the straw. "Barbara loved strawberry. She was my best friend in Virginia."

"It's great to have a best friend." I smile at Debbie to make sure they both get my point.

"Yeah, I guess." Suzanne glances at me. "But since we've moved so much, I'm always saying goodbye to friends."

Debbie gives me an isn't-that-sad-and-try-to-understand look. I bet Suzanne doesn't make friends, she steals them.

As Debbie reaches for a napkin, she stops and says "What's this?" She picks up the paper bag with the Beatles stuff in it and looks at my drawing. "It looks like a rat. But it has long hair."

I grab the bag back. "Yes, it is a rat. A big rat." I glare into Suzanne's amber eyes. I need to get away. Right now.

I purposely look up at the clock above the counter. "Oh no.

It's almost 4:30 and I'm late. Mom will have a cow." I toss Debbie's two card packs onto the counter and hop off the stool.

I race out of Woolworth's into the cold and run through town, my heart pounding. When I stop to catch my breath, I pull the Beatles stuff out of the paper bag with my drawing of The Rat Fink, rip the bag in half, crumple it up, and throw it into a garbage can.

If only getting rid of a real Rat Fink was that easy.

10 • Mrs. Egan's *Atelier*

Weeks and weeks have dragged by, but today is finally the day for my first Thursday afternoon painting lesson. And I've earned it. I've spent my Saturdays at Mrs. Zabriskie's doing chores like dusting her ceramic chicken collection (she has 103! I counted), carrying laundry baskets up and down to her creepy cobwebbed basement, and picking up bags of Fluffy's stinky poop in the backyard. But it's been so worth it if it means I'll learn to paint and triumph over Bill.

My chores have meant less time with Debbie, and her French Club has meant less time with me. The Rat Fink now eats lunch at our table. She and Debbie sometimes drift into French gibberish that leaves me out. If I'm lucky enough to know some Beatles gossip, I can recapture Debbie's ear for awhile. But then The Rat Fink brings up some French recipe she tried, like for something called "keesh," whatever that is, and she's got Debbie's attention again. It's exhausting—all this competing. I'm starting to wonder if the prize is really worth it.

* * * * *

School moved in agonizing super-slow motion today. At the sound of the 3:00 bell, I bolt out of the building, race home, change my clothes, and fly out the door to Mrs. Egan's house for my very first painting lesson.

Mrs. Egan's house is a one of a kind creation. It may be the same size and shape of all the other split-level houses in our development, but it has its own unique attitude. With its lemony-yellow paint, purple trim, and a red front door, it pops like a van Gogh painting that's rebelling against all the neutral-colored houses around it.

When I knock, the red front door swings open. Wearing a black turtleneck and slacks, silver beads the size of ping pong balls, and a turquoise and silver belt buckle, Mrs. Egan is a work of art herself. Her dark hair is pulled high into a swingy ponytail and her bangs are cut straight across, an inch above her shaped, black eyebrows and lined brown eyes. Long hoops of silver hang from her ears.

"Ah, Remmy Rinaldi! Welcome to Atelier Egan," she says, flashing a big smile and waving her arm with a flourish.

My face must have a giant question mark on it because she quickly adds, "Oh, *atelier* means 'workshop' in French."

French. Well, at least Debbie will know that word and it should impress her that I'm painting in an *atelier*.

I step into the Egan living room and it's like a Mondrian geometrical abstract painting—the complete opposite of my sweet-as-apple-pie Norman-Rockwell-decor house.

All the walls are crisp white. The sofa and chairs are like upholstered Legos with sharp angles and low rectangular shapes in primary colors. One fabric chair is shaped like an orange butterfly. A huge poster is framed on the wall. Its all drips and spots and squiggles and slashes in blacks and reds and oranges and grays. I'm not sure what it's supposed to be, but it's cool, man, real cool.

I hang my jacket and scarf on a hook next to two other kids' jackets. One jacket is very familiar. Too familiar.

"Grab your supplies and let's go upstairs, dear." Bangle bracelets jangle on Mrs. Egan's wrist as she motions to the attic stairs with another dramatic sweep of her arm. She's helping me keep my secret from Dad by letting me hide my art supplies in her garage. "How can I deny such passion?" she had said, pressing her hands to her heart. "There is no greater joy than seeing young talent bloom."

I stop at the top of the attic stairs, close my eyes, and inhale. Ah, the smell of oil paint and linseed oil—the smell of art. It's like the salty breeze of the ocean to a surfer or the aroma of cinnamon and chocolate to a baker.

Wood rafters hold up the ceiling and skylights brighten the attic room. Four easels are set up in a semi-circle around a table. So this is what an *atelier* looks like. I'm thrilled to be here.

"Remmy, Bill tell me he's an old friend of yours," Mrs. Egan says.

And there goes the thrill.

"Yes, we go way back." I fake a big smile and nod at Bill.

"How're you doing, Miss Rembrandt?" Bill rubs the top of his crew cut head. "So nice to have you join us."

The last thing I want to do is spend an extra two hours a week with Bill, but my Spark is more important than my hate of him.

Bill chuckles and goes back to setting up his palette.

Another girl sits at an easel. Karen Englebert is humming something that sounds classical, but stops and gives me a friendly wave. She has a bubble of red curly hair and black horn-rimmed glasses, but it's odd to see her not carrying a violin case like she always does at school.

"Hey Karen." I smile and wave back. "You're not going to serenade us with your violin?"

She laughs. "I might accidently try to play using my brush instead of a bow. What a mess."

I hear footsteps running up the stairs. It must be the last student.

"And Remmy," says Mrs. Egan, "You must know Peter McCleary."

I spin around. "Peter?!!"

Holy Whistler's Mother! Why didn't I know he's taking these lessons?

Bill covers his mouth, holding in a laugh.

I look into Peter's eyes, and am sucked into that pool of

hazeliscious dreaminess while at the same time panicking at their closeness.

"Yeah, hi Remmy," he says. The tops of his ears turn red.

I back away. Suddenly, my feet tangle, my arms fly up into the air, and I tumble into the clutches of an attacking wooden creature.

"Remmy!" Mrs. Egan runs over to rescue me from the grasp of an easel.

Bill and Peter scream with laughter, while Karen politely hides her giggles behind her hand.

Curses! Some great impression I've made at my first lesson. What a klutz! I avoid everyone's eyes, especially those dreamy hazeliscious ones, while I right the easel.

I can tell Mrs. Egan's squeezed lips are holding in a laugh. She quickly recovers and says, "Okay, all of you. Cool it. Just worry about your own supplies, and finish setting up so we can start this colorful still life."

She turns on spotlights that cast highlights and shadows on a yellow bowl filled with red apples and green pears. All the colors make electrical charges that ignite in my brain and travel through my arms, preparing my hands to paint. I'm here. I made it!

I put on one of Dad's old white office shirts as a painting smock, which still has the faint minty scent of his Aqua Velva aftershave. At first, the scent takes me to our kitchen in the morning as Dad breezes by, leaving for work. But then my stomach does flip flops because the shirt smells like guilt—my guilt for going behind his back.

God has Ten Commandments, including the fifth: Honor thy mother and thy father. Since Mom knows about this plan, maybe I'm only breaking a half a Commandment? I'll have to avoid our dining room, so those Three Heavenly Catholics' eyes don't judge me.

My guilt is quickly replaced by excitement as I open my new, old paint box that Mom found at a rummage sale. The chipped and scratched wooden box has a faded patina of paint stains and looks like it's seen decades and decades of painting. It has that oil smell deep in its pores. I swear I can actually feel the spirit of the artist who owned it, whoever he was.

My hand glides across the shiny-new, unopened tubes of paint. Ultramarine blue, thalo green, lemon yellow light, cadmium red, burnt sienna, cerulean blue, yellow ochre, raw umber. Juicy, gorgeous colors! I grab the tube of alizarin crimson, ready to squeeze out a palette full of colors, but Mrs. Egan stops me.

"Sorry, Remmy. I'm starting you out with the basics of shadow and light, like the others did back in September. Just put out ivory black and titanium white. You'll do the entire painting in tones of gray."

"Tones of gray?" Tones of gray! I worked my caboose off at Mrs. Zabriskie's earning money just to paint in tones of gray? This isn't why I'm here. My painting needs to explode with color. Now. Like van Gogh. Instead, my painting will look like a plain old Jon Gnagy drawing demonstration on our black and white TV.

Bill snickers at me and whispers, "We all have to start somewhere, Miss Rembrandt. Be patient. You might catch up to the rest of us."

I frown at him and then look over at dreamy Peter and catch his hazeliscious eyes. I lower my head and smile at him, like I've seen Debbie flirt. He quickly looks away and the tips of his ears turn red again. Phooey! Was that sympathy in his eyes or just pathetic pity?

I reluctantly squeeze out blobs of white and black on my palette to make my tones of gray. I remind myself that van Gogh painted "The Potato Eaters" early in his career. It's a dark painting of peasants huddling under a lantern, having their meal. There's hardly any color in it, mostly muddy browns. I guess Vincent had to start somewhere, too. So if it was good enough for Vincent, it's good enough for me.

During the lesson, Mrs. Egan flits from one easel to the next, like an excited parrot, giving directions on composition, proportion, mixing colors (or tones of gray, in my case), brush strokes, shadows, highlights. She's a great teacher!

Did Mrs. Egan want to be a famous artist when she was twelve like me? What were her dreams? Guess it doesn't matter now since she's just a mom who looks like an artist. But she does know how to teach us so she has to be a real artist. The attic walls have prints of famous paintings, but none of her paintings are hanging. Does she have any? Where are they? What do they look like? I bet Nancy Drew could figure this out. Yeah, *The Mystery of the Invisible Artist. The Clue of the Covert Canvas.* Too bad Nancy's fictional because I want answers.

As I concentrate on making the apples and pears appear on my canvas, I forget I'm working in black and white. I also forget about classical Karen, dreamy Peter, and goofball Bill. With Mrs. Egan's guidance, my flat shapes become dimensional fruit, and look good enough to eat, except who wants to eat gray fruit?

But that really isn't the point. I'm finally painting in oils, fanning My Spark, and am one step closer to winning the Art Awards!

11 • Snowflop

At 7 a.m., I bolt awake and check my window. It's barely light out. Sure enough, like the weather girl said, we've been hit by a March snow storm overnight, but it's much more snow than was predicted. Yippee!!

I turn on my transistor radio very, very low to listen to the reading of school closings, keeping my fingers crossed. After three agonizingly-long minutes, the announcer finally says Benjamin Franklin Junior High. Yes! Snow day!

Is there anything more fantastic than a snow day?

But the schoolwork-free day of fun has to wait until I first do my job and shovel at Mrs. Zabriskie's. Even though it isn't Saturday, this is an emergency responsibility and a windfall for my painting fund.

My giant teddy bear, Little Joe, slouches sleepily against the

WOW!Wall. I arrange him in my bed, and pull the covers over him and tuck and push until the lump resembles a sleeping me.

I peek out my bedroom. Good.Mom and Dad's door is shut, so they're still asleep.

With the stealth of a cat burglar, I tiptoe down the stairs, making sure to step over the sixth step that creaks. I take my red snow jacket out of the closet and turn it inside out to the black lining. I stuff all my hair into one of Dad's wool caps and slip into my snow boots. My disguise is complete.

When I open the back door, I breathe in the cold air of money, and wade through the deep snow.

The early dawn light casts cool shadows on the snowy houses and streets. It's as if the whole scene has been painted using only tones of gray, like at Mrs. Egan's. It's all shapes and volumes of shades. I'd rather be painting, but I'm heading off to work so I can afford to paint.

I go right to the shed so I don't disturb Mrs. Zabriskie, and especially Fluffy, and start shoveling. And shoveling and shoveling and shoveling.

The sun is fully up by the time I finally dig my way to the front door. Mrs. Zabriskie's glasses peer out through the lace curtains and she opens the door. After all those Saturdays, Fluffy still greets me with a deep mean growl.

"I see the early bird has caught the worm," Mrs. Zabriskie chuckles. "That was a big job, Rosie. You're my strong little snow angel."

With that, she puts four dollars in my jacket pocket. "See you

71

Saturday." She closes her door to the cold wintery day.

Four bucks! Yep, I sure caught my worm.

When I reach Meadow Lane, screaming boys are flying down the white street on sleds. They zoom past me, whooping and hollering like wild banshees, and smash into snow banks to stop. They leap up, grab their sleds, and race back up to the top of the hill.

One of the snow-covered figures stops in front of me.

"Miss Rembrandt?" Bill pants steam out his mouth. "I didn't recognize you."

He snatches my cap off, and I grab it back.

"That's the idea, Sherlock. Hopefully my father won't either." I shove my hair back into the cap and check my sleeping house at the bottom of the hill.

"Pretty sneaky. Didn't think you really had the guts to pull a fast one on your father."

"A girl's gotta do what a girl's gotta do," I reply.

In a weak moment, I had bragged to Bill about paying for my painting lessons myself so my father wouldn't know about them. I wanted to show Bill I'm a girl of action and determination. Now I regret letting him on my secret. He could even blackmail me if I'm not careful.

Bill tugs on my arm. "C'mon with us. Let's see how much guts you really have."

I hesitate, imagining what evil trick Bill might play on me. But it feels so great to be outside and not in school that I follow. We traipse up to the top of the hill, and boys get into position to race.

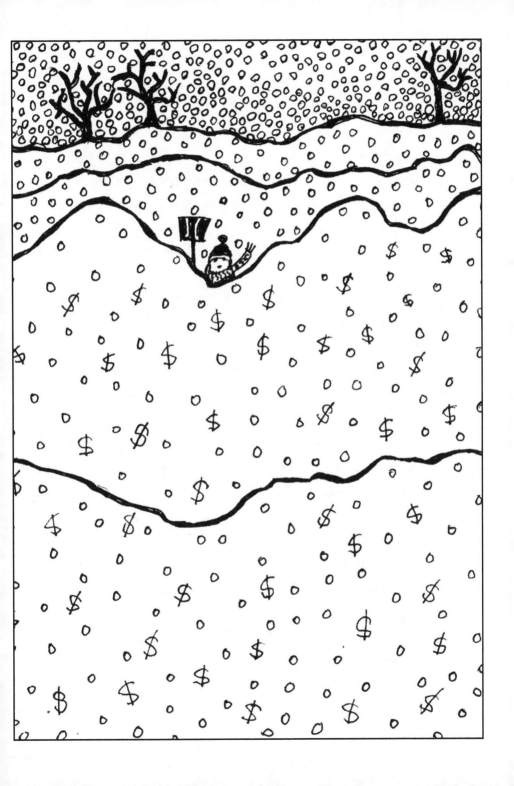

I look out over the snowy neighborhood. Fathers are starting to come out to shovel their driveways.

"Hey, let's go," Bill calls to me. He's lying down on his sled. "Jump on my back and hold on."

The sun makes a bright glare on the snow so I shade my eyes with my mittened hand. Yikes. The hill now seems much steeper from a sled's-eye view.

"Um, no. Go ahead. I'll watch from up here." I take a few steps back.

"What happened to those guts? What are you? Little Miss Chicken?" Bill clucks.

"Oh yeah? I'll show you who's chicken!" I take a running start, jump onto Bill's back, and the sled hurtles down the hill. Terrified and thrilled, I clutch Bill's shoulders, and howl. The spray of snow stings my face, but I laugh.

Another sledder veers towards us, and Bill cuts to the left. I close my eyes and scream, clutching his head. He skids to the right and back to the left in a blinding cloud of snow until we hit something and get flipped off the sled.

"Cripes! You crazy delinquents! You tryin' to kill me?!"

I sure know that voice.

Bill jumps up. "I'm so sorry, Mr. Rinaldi! She grabbed my head. I couldn't see."

I look up from my landing spot in the snow bank. Dad's eyebrows shoot up as he realizes who he's looking at.

"Ro-sel-la Ma-ri-a Ri-nal-di! Inside!"

12 • My Sentence—Now and Future

The sound of forks and knives clinks against plates. Jesus, Good Pope John XXIII, and JFK frown at me in disgust, as does Dad.

He had sentenced me to spend the rest of the snow day in my room. My Super Secret Sketchbook kept me company as I doodled and contemplated my wrongdoing. I regret the "wrong" of wiping out Dad, but I have to admit I enjoyed the thrill of the "doing," thanks to Bill.

Now it's time to face my victim and find out if my punishment will continue.

"What were you thinking?" Dad asks. "You could have killed me."

I look down at my plate of untouched meat loaf drowned in a lake of catsup.

"You snuck out to play with those boys like a common street urchin. You're a young lady now, not some wild hooligan."

"Yes, sir."

"And you need to behave like a young lady."

Young lady, young lady.

I glance at Mom. She nods with a crooked smile.

"You're grounded for a week," Dad decrees. "Come home immediately after school and stay in your room. And don't even think about sneaking down to the playroom to watch TV.

"A week? But I'll miss Mrs. ...." I slam my hand across my mouth. Mom's mouth drops open.

"You'll miss who?" Dad leans forward.

"Um...I'll miss...uh....Miss Pipp's poetry reading after school. On Thursday."

"Poetry. A useless art." He resumes eating his metabola.

Art. Useless.

"Isn't grounding me for a whole week kind of excessive? What if I have to go to the library after school to research a project? That could hurt my grade. And what about missing Catechism tomorrow? Isn't that a sin?"

Dad doesn't look up from his meat loaf, but shakes his head.

The main problem, the tragedy of all tragedies, is that I'll miss Mrs. Egan's lesson on Thursday, but Dad doesn't know that. His punishment is much more painful than he even realizes.

I poke at my meat loaf and jab lima beans into the top of my mashed potatoes to look like trees on a snowy mountain.

The Three Heavenly Catholics on the wall now have

sympathy in their eyes, like they believe in my dream. They give me courage. I touch my opal and look at Mom.

"Oh Mom, I got an A on my landscape project for art class. Mr. Neel says I have a special talent with pastels." At least he encourages my Spark.

"That's terrific, sweetie." Mom lights up. "You do have a gift, maybe even a family gift." She gives Dad an odd, scolding look.

He ignores it and begins lecture number two.

"I'm telling you, Rosella," Dad says, waving his fork at me. "The only talent you'll need is to find a nice boy to marry and enjoy a happy life."

A smile appears on his face which is not a good sign. I brace myself for what else might be coming next.

"Until then, concentrate on your home economics classes and practice your typing. After high school, you can go to secretarial school. That's what your mother did and look at her wonderful life."

Mom blushes and smiles a *wonderful* smile. I picture myself chained to a *wonderful* typewriter and shutter.

"You could go into nursing if you didn't faint at the sight of blood," Dad chuckles.

He's right. Just hearing the word "blood" makes me woozy and I hold onto the edge of the table.

"Or teaching! Teaching is the perfect profession for girls," he proclaims and shoves a forkful of lima beans into his mouth.

Mom nods. "Or, sweetie, you could teach art." Mom gives me a hopeful smile and I return it. "You could share your gift."

Dad coughs and lima bean bullets spray the table.

"Angela! Gift or no gift, my daughter will not become an artist!"

Holy Grandma Moses! Am I doomed? Are these the only options in a girl's life?

Imagine being a secretary, sitting in front of a typewriter, my fingers going tappity-tap... tappity-tap...ding, all day long. My Spark would be smothered in an office.

And the absolute last thing I want to do is be back in school teaching a roomful of goofball Bills and stuck-up Rat Finks until some Prince Charming marries me so I can keep the castle clean and mend his tights.

Maybe before marriage I can be an airline stewardess. Yeah, then I can see the paintings and statues and cathedrals all over Europe.

Ugh, the future is too over-whelming.

* * * * *

After dinner, I trudge upstairs. Instead of going into my bedroom, I quietly sneak into what used to be Nonna's room and is now the guest room.

So much of Nonna is still in this room, even though she's been in Heaven for six years. There's a faint smell of moth balls coming from the closet. I fiddle with the dials on the oversized wooden radio on the dresser, and run my hand across the lacey runner she crocheted. Above the bed is a plaque of the Madonna and Child

looking kindly at me as if they understand what I'm going through.

I pick up the ornate gold frame from the nightstand. In it is a sepia photograph of young Nonna with her husband and their three small children—Dad, Aunt Teresa, and Uncle Vinnie, all standing stiffly and seriously. I put the frame back without taking my eyes off Nonna's face.

This grounding will make it even harder for me to catch up with the other kids at Mrs. Egan's. After working in tones of gray for a few weeks, Mrs. Egan moved me up to working in brown tones with thin overlays of color. She calls it glazing, and I've worked that way for two weeks, finally using at least some color. It's a pretty cool technique.

But on Thursday, I was going to graduate up to full color and try to catch up to the others. I'd show Bill that this girl can paint! I'd swoop and stroke and dab and blend and dazzle. But now it will have to wait. Drat!

Hey, did Bill plan all this—the sledding and wiping out Dad— just so I would trail behind him at Mrs. Egan's and lose the Art Awards contest? He must be even more afraid of competition from me than I realized.

Who am I kidding? As evil as he is, I don't think Bill has the brains to pull off that complicated a plot. It was just my dumb bad luck.

I climb on Nonna's soft bed, and curl up under her woolen afghan. I pretend Nonna is holding me like she used to, gently singing in Italian. Her songs always made me forget pain, like when I scraped my knee roller skating or that time I lost my Betsy

Wetsy. But now I'm feeling a different kind of pain that's hard to fix with just a melody.

I remember coloring in this room, and hearing Nonna say, "Brava, cara. Giacomo would be so proud."

Giocomo. My grandfather. A man I never knew. I look at his face in the old photo. Why would he be proud?

13 • The Portrait

I try to put my grounding to good use by drawing self-portraits in my Super Secret Sketchbook as a way to practice drawing people. As much as I love Mrs. Egan's lessons, we've only painted still lifes and I want to be more impressively versatile so I can win the contest.

I sit in front of a mirror and put on hats like van Gogh, and make silly expressions like Rembrandt, and try to draw myself. But it's really hard to look at yourself in a mirror, then look down and draw, then look back in the mirror. All my self-portraits come out horrible—mismatched eyes, noses too small or too big or too crooked, lopsided sad or angry mouths. And hair! How can anyone draw hair without it looking like spaghetti or mashed potatoes?

I need a better model than myself once my grounding is over. And I know just the person.

* * * * *

This week, my after-school time is finally back to normal and I've convinced Debbie to come over to model for me and to get some quality best-friend alone time with her. After all, who knows what kind of evil spell The Rat Fink has cast on her while I was serving time locked in my room? My pencil is a wand that will magically eradicate any wicked sorcery that has trapped Debbie.

"I missed you last week, although I was pretty busy with French Club," Debbie says.

French Club. Ugh.

"I really missed you, too. But we're together now and can make up for lost time. How are things going with Jacques?"

Debbie's eyes get googly. "The other day I bumped into him in the hallway accidentally on purpose! But he started to tumble and I had to grab him before he hit the floor." She giggles. "He may have said a bad word in French, but I haven't looked it up yet."

Debbie's tactics are not very subtle, but I have to admire her determination.

"Maybe a gentler approach will be better next time."

She shrugs her shoulders. "I suppose so, but I'm getting impatient."

"Well, he's the fool for not recognizing what a gem you are."

I give Debbie my remember-you're-my-best-friend smile and she smiles back a little weakly, but still a smile.

"Let's get started." I pull my desk chair over near the window for the best light. "Sit here and try not to move."

"Well, I can't guarantee. I've never posed before."

Debbie plops into the chair and smooths her flip. I get her to sit up straight, pose her arms across her lap, and tell her to look directly at me.

"Give me that I'm-thinking-of-Jacques smile and you'll do great." I turn on my record player in hopes that the Beatles will keep Debbie relaxed and not bored.

Drawing Debbie instead of myself in a mirror is so much better. It let's me concentrate on capturing what I see. As I draw in my sketchbook, I feel a special force guiding my hand so that all the features of her face and all her inner personality come together in a true representation of all she is to me—my very best friend.

But, after seven minutes, she's squirming and twisting like she's riding the Tilt-a-Whirl. As soon as I draw a shadow, her head moves and the shadow changes shape. Then her smile droops and her dimple disappears. Her eyes look away. She checks her flip with her hand.

Grrrrr. Did Mona Lisa give Leonardo such a hard time?

"Deb, come on. Sit still. Pleeeeze..."

She frowns at me, jumps off the chair, kicks her legs and swings her arms. "My rear end is totally numb, needles are zipping up my arms, and my face muscles are sick of smiling." She crosses her arms. "Aren't you done yet? Let me see."

I slam the sketchbook against my chest to hide the drawing from her.

"Hey, listen to what the Beatles are singing...'it won't be

long'." I nod my head over at the record player.

"But the Beatles make me want to dance." Deb wiggles and waves her arms to the beat and jumps around my bedroom.

"I'm so close to finished and this could be one of my best drawings ever. I swear. No more than five more minutes." And I mean it. With this portrait in the Art Awards, I'll beat out that showoff Bill for sure.

Deb slows down her crazy dance and sways while checking her flip again, not that it would move anyway with all that hair spray on it.

"You know, if it's such a good portrait, you should let me give it to Jacques."

Debbie sits down on the chair and gets back into position. "That portrait would earn me some points with him and he could look at me whenever he wants. Oh, he is so *magnifique*." In spite of her lack of progress with Jacques, she still gets that sparkle in her eye and the perfect smile on her face.

I better capture that expression before it disappears again. I feel the special force return and my pencil races around the paper, adding details and softening shadows until my drawing is perfect and I know I really am finished. No uneven eyes. No bulbous nose. No twisted mouth. Even with all of Debbie's fidgeting, this portrait will be a perfect addition to my Art Awards portfolio.

I hold my sketchbook away from me so I can get a good look without Debbie seeing it. "Wow, this is so good. You're going to love it."

I've totally impressed myself.

Debbie flies off the chair. "Well, let me see! Come on, come on!"

I turn around the sketchbook to face her. "Look!"

Debbie freezes for a couple of seconds. Then her smile disappears, her eyes get super wide, and her mouth drops open.

"THAT'S NOT ME!! What have you done? That's a terrible drawing! Is that what I look like to you? A big fatso? A blimp? A hippo?"

What? What is she seeing that I'm not seeing? This is all wrong.

"No, no, Deb, not a big fatso." I can hardly speak. I look at my drawing and back at my friend and try to choke out an answer. "You're not fat. A little plump maybe, but not fat."

I show her the drawing again. "And look, see your pretty smile and dimple? And how I caught the sparkle in your eyes? Like you're thinking about Jacques?"

But her actual eyes are now filled with tears. "How could you do this to me?! You are so mean and you're a terrible artist and you'll never win that stupid contest!"

Deb spins around and bumps against the record player which lets out a huge screech as the player needle scratches across the record and the Beatles stop singing. She races out of my room and down the stairs.

I hear voices and the front door slams.

"Rosella! Get down here!"

Curses! Dad's home. I just insulted my best friend with the best drawing of my life and she just ruined my best album. And

now I have to answer to Dad about doing nothing wrong.

"Rosella!"

I slowly inch down the stairs one step at a time until I'm in front of my parents but keep my eyes glued to the floor.

"What did you do to Debbie? Look at me. I've never seen her cry like that." Dad crosses his arms and waits for an answer. Mom tugs at the pearls around her neck and keeps quiet.

"Well, uh..." I look away. "Oh, it was just silly girl stuff. You know, like she thinks John is the best Beatle and I think Paul is and..."

"What's this?"

Ack! My Super Secret Sketchbook is still in my hand.

Dad grabs the sketchbook. He looks at the drawing of Debbie and grunts.

Mom cranes her neck to get a good look. "Oh sweetie, that's wonderful. You really caught her expression and your technique is lovely."

"I drew that portrait of Debbie and she hated it and said she looked like a fatso and a blimp and a hippo and how could I do that to her but I think it's great and she's just stupid." Words spill out of me like I don't want them in my mouth and tears sting my eyes.

"We never use the word stupid." Dad waves the sketchbook at me. "And see what I told you? Art can hurt people. It can cause a great deal of pain. See? Your artwork hurt Debbie."

"And what about me? Debbie hurt me. She thinks I'm a terrible artist." Friends don't think that way about friends, especially when one friend has the Spark.

Dad lets my sketchbook drop to the floor. It hurts as much as if he had dropped me.

He stomps into the living room, throws himself into his chair, lights a cigarette, and snaps open the newspaper.

I hold the opal on my necklace. Dad's attitude makes me even more determined to follow My Spark. To be a great artist. A famous one. And I'll start by showing him—and Debbie—who is going to win the Art Awards.

Mom picks up my sketchbook and sighs.

"You have true talent, sweetie." Mom whispers and hands me the sketchbook. "Don't give up." She frowns and marches into the living room.

I look again at the plump portrait. It is Debbie all over, hippo or no hippo.

As I trudge back upstairs, I hear muffled voices from the living room. Is Mom yelling?

14 • Trying to Make Sense

Instead of retreating to my bedroom, I go into Nonna's room, sit on her bed, and look into her eyes in the old family photo. Nonna comforts me while I hug my Super Secret Sketchbook. She would have loved all my sketchbooks—even more than she loved my coloring.

I look at Debbie's portrait again. Her twinkly eyes and her smile with that dimple. I could probably draw her face without her even being in the room. It's as familiar to me as my own face.

What is going on? Life feels all jumbly and cracking. My best friend is chasing a French (Canadian) boy, spending more and more time with that Francophile Rat Fink, and has no real appreciation for my Spark. We've been best friends since kindergarten when we moved into our brand-new houses right next door to each other. And now? Has this portrait actually damaged our friendship? And

Dad has already planned my whole future. Is he right about the destructive power of art?

I hear heavy footsteps on the stairs, and quickly wipe tears off my face. I hold my breath as Dad passes by. Whew, I don't think I could handle another lecture. But then he walks back and peeks into Nonna's room.

"Oh, there you are. May I join you?" Dad says, with a crooked smile.

I shrug my shoulders and put my sketchbook behind me on the bed.

He sits down next to me, and examines his hands for a while, not looking at me.

Finally Dad says, "Your mother has been pushing me to talk to you and I..."

He fidgets, then lets out a big breath that smells of cigarettes. I've never seen Dad this hesitant. He's always so sure of himself in that Henry VIII kingly way. But this time, something is different.

"Rosella, I see that you do have talent. I'm not blind," he says.

Wow, is he starting to understand my dream?

I touch my opal and take my chances on breaking the wall between us, or at least drilling a peep hole into it.

"I really really want to be an artist. I am an artist," I say. "This is so important to me. I have my Spark."

Dad sighs and finally looks at me. His strong will has returned to his eyes.

"Talent isn't everything. That's only part of an artist's life."

Dad and I look away from each other. There is a long, long

pause. I can almost hear my pounding heart.

"Look. I've worked hard to give you and your mother a secure and happy life. I only want the best for your future. Not some struggling artist's life." Dad's voice has a little wobble in it. "You need to be taken care of. You'll need a husband and family of your own someday."

"Sure I want a family, but I can still live my dream."

Dad shakes his head. "Not in today's world. Why fight your God-given nature, Rosella? Can't you enjoy the benefits of just being a girl?"

"So this is really all about me just being a girl?"

"Yes...And no."

Well that's a big help. I wait.

"Rosella," he says. "I haven't talked to you much about my father, your grandfather."

"Giocomo?"

"Yes, Giocomo." Dad doesn't smile when he says the name. He picks up the old photo in the gold frame, and silently stares at it.

"My father had been a tailor in Italy," he finally says. "Then he and Nonna immigrated to New York City in 1912 to find a better life. But it turned out to be very difficult for all the Italian, Jewish, and Eastern European immigrants who flooded into the city. They lived in crowded tenement apartments and survived as best they could while they built new lives. Fortunately, my father was able to find work because his tailoring skills were so fine."

Nonna had told me only a few stories about that time period.

"My father was also an accomplished painter," Dad says.

"Oh." I suck in my breath. Nonna didn't mention *that* story!

I can't believe it. I did inherit my art genes and they're flickering right now.

Dad continues. "When the Great Depression hit the country, we all suffered. My father found some work as a tailor, but not enough. We needed more money."

I don't dare crack Dad's Great Depression joke about Aunt Teresa's girdle.

Dad puts the photo back on the nightstand and paces. "In spite of our financial hardships, every night after dinner, my father would pick up his paint box, and go paint in a warehouse space he shared with other artists."

Dad stops and wipes an eye. "And your poor Nonna would put on her coat, wrap a shawl over her head, and take the subway uptown. After taking care of three children and a home all day, she would clean offices at night."

Anger rises in his voice. "I was the oldest. So after Nonna left, I cleaned up the kitchen, and put Teresa and Vinnie to bed. When I went to bed myself, all I could think about was my poor mother scrubbing floors just so my father could go paint. I hated him for that. He was so selfish."

Now I understand.

"Oh, Dad, I'm so sorry. Poor Nonna."

"Yeah, poor Nonna."

And poor Dad.

Dad goes to stand in front of a small painting on the far wall—

an old city street scene, busy with carts, swarms of people, and fire escapes like spider webs clinging to the sides of buildings. The energetic brushstrokes make the neighborhood feel alive and vibrant. I've always loved this painting.

"My father painted this," Dad says. "The only painting Nonna was able to save all these years."

Of course!

"It's beautiful," I say.

"Yes, it is. But our life wasn't beautiful. I want you to have a beautiful life." Dad turns and looks at me with stern eyes. "And being an artist won't make that possible for you. Now I hope you now fully understand and will respect my wishes." Dad leaves the room.

Wow. This is a lot to take in. Almost too much.

Sure I can understand how difficult Dad's life was and the sacrifices Nonna made. I can't imagine having to live like that.

But there was some beauty. I smile at my grandfather's painting. Art added the beauty.

Dad's history isn't giving me permission to be an artist. But it's also not convincing me to give up my dream. Life for an artist during The Great Depression can't be compared to life now.

I clutch my Super Secret Sketchbook to my chest and carry it protectively back to my room.

On the WOW!WALL I see two silly happy faces—the photos of me and Debbie in the Woolworth's photo booth. Best friends forever.

Is that friendship still alive? Tomorrow at school will tell.

15 • Chasing Forgiveness

The next day, I only see quick glimpses of Debbie scooting through school. The situation is worse than I feared. I need to catch her and make things right. But how? Agree with her I'm a terrible artist? Or try to convince her I'm still learning and apologize?

But confronting Debbie is impossible. I follow her through the hallways. If I zig, she zags. If I zip, she zooms. I spend all day trying to catch her, like that crazy coyote chasing the speedy roadrunner.

In social studies, Debbie won't make eye contact with me and dashes out the room as soon as the bell sounds.

In the cafeteria, she and The Rat Fink huddle together whispering and giggling. I don't dare go near.

In home ec, she concentrates on her sewing project, never

letting her eyes leave the sewing machine. Again, she beats me out the door when the bell rings.

Like that wily coyote, I never catch her.

* * * * *

I sit on my bed with my math book open. Math homework is hard enough to do when I'm not agonizing over my best friend. The numbers bounce around the page and I don't have enough concentration to tame them back into place.

I give up. Maybe drawing will calm me and help me focus. I retrieve my Super Secret Sketchbook from its hiding place in the closet.

I flip through the pages, but I end up only staring at Debbie's portrait. It's still the best thing I've ever drawn. But I've never seen Debbie so angry, not even when her little brother stole her Ken doll and painted a blue mustache on him. Her anger at me is so colossal that I may never get her friendship back. Not ever.

Hoping to glimpse into the future, I grab the Magic 8 Ball and shake it, since it did such a great job of predicting I'd find a way to make painting money.

"Will Debbie be my friend again?"

I flip the ball over and the triangle comes into focus.

"Not likely."

"That's the best you can do, you indecisive ball? Try harder. How can I get her forgiveness?" I shake and shake and shake but don't even look for the answer in the triangle. The more I shake, the more tears stream down my face. I throw the ball onto my bed and go back to my sketchbook.

My best friend smiles at me, but I can't look at the portrait anymore and I rip it out of my sketchbook. I'm upset enough to crumple it up, but I can't destroy my best work. No, I'll hide it safely away. Maybe this disaster will blow over. I bet Debbie and I will be laughing about the whole thing next week.

Yes, this will just be temporary. I take the portrait down to the basement, wrap it in sheets of tissue paper and zip it into a sweater bag which I lock in a suitcase that I put into a trunk that I hide behind the stairs of the basement. Safe and sound until our friendship is restored.

16 • Secrets In The Garage

It's Thursday afternoon and Mrs. Egan's attic is much too quiet. Usually Karen's humming breaks the silence, but she isn't here yet. Peter's playing in a basketball tournament, so he's not coming, which is just as well because I don't have to force myself to avoid those hazeliscious eyes.

So it's just me and Bill.

Ten days after the incident, Debbie is still avoiding me. Our friendship may be over because of my art and the thought of losing her to that Rat Fink is killing me. Add to that the burden of knowing Dad's painful history, and it could be that I should accept that my Spark is totally messing up my life.

Bill taps a rhythm with his brushes on the easel and bops his head. Who does he think he is? Ringo? Maybe he does, because his crew cut has grown out and his hair is beginning to reach his eyebrows and curl over his ears.

My palette's set up with the full spectrum of colors since Mrs. Egan feels I've progressed to a level that understands color relationships, like how putting a touch of blue next to its complimentary color orange increases the orange's vibrancy. "Remmy dear," she had said. "Your use of color is so instinctual. It's as if you have an inner spirit guiding you." I smile and think of my grandfather.

Bill stops drumming. The new silence feels as if a huge pillow has muffled the attic, making the thoughts in my brain extra loud. I pretend to look for a missing paint tube in my box as a way to ignore Bill. I rub the worn wood of the box, admiring my rainbow of tubes.

Bill coughs as we wait for Mrs. Egan. He obviously sees that my friendship with Debbie has dissolved. Should I ask him if he thinks art is more important than friendship? As if I can't guess his answer.

A jangle of bangles announces that Mrs. Egan is finally coming up the stairs.

"That was our Karen on the phone," she calls out. "She has a miserable sore throat and is totally distraught she won't be coming. Poor thing sounded like a tone-deaf bull frog."

Mrs. Egan steps into the attic and frowns. "Great Gauguin's ghost! It's as quiet as a cemetery at midnight in here." She quickly turns on the hi-fi and familiar voices fill the room. "That's more like it!"

I agree! Yeah, yeah, yeah.

"Hey, Mrs. E," Bill says, "you like the Beatles? My parents think they're the pits."

"Well, I think they're a unique and refreshing change to my ears. The music world certainly could use a little revolution." She sweeps her arm across her in a dramatic gesture, but her hand smacks into a large old easel.

"Ooww! Sugar! This old monstrosity is always in the way." She rubs her hand, frowning at the easel. "I don't even use this relic. Look. I still need to pull together more objects for our still life. Would you two carry this easel out to the garage for me? Be careful. It's very heavy, so don't injure those talented hands."

Mrs. Egan sails down the stairs to look for props, and Bill jumps to his feet, doing his manly duty and taking charge.

"You heard her, Miss Rembrandt. I'll carry the bottom and go down the stairs backwards. I've got the muscle power." Bill flexes his arm and makes a feeble muscle. Most of his muscle is in his head.

Then I notice something.

"Hey, didn't you have a sprained wrist?" I remember seeing it taped up when he was talking to some guys from the lacrosse team a few days ago.

"Oh, yeah." He massages his wrist. "It healed really quickly. Too bad I missed lacrosse tryouts."

Yeah, too bad, my foot. He's always finding the perfect scam to avoid sports tryouts, while I'd give anything to tryout for a sport if girls were allowed.

The easel is super heavy and clumsy like a huge uncooperative robot, but we manage to wrestle it down the attic stairs in lurches and stops, yelling orders at each other all the way. We maneuver it through the house, almost sending the dining room Sputnik chandelier into outer space. We put down the easel a few feet from the garage.

Bill flings up the door and garage is crammed full of stuff, except for the space left by Mr. Egan's car.

"Wow," Bill says. "And she thinks this easel will fit in here? There's more room in my locker at school."

I quickly step in front of a stack of paintings against one wall.

"Hey, aren't these yours?" He pushes me aside. "Yeah, I recognize that naïve technique."

"You're just jealous."

Bill shrugs and goes to the opposite side of the garage. He stretches to look over a stack of boxes, which is easy when you're built like a giraffe.

"Let's pull these out and see if the easel can squeeze behind here," he says.

Dust clouds fill the air as we tug and push boxes around. No one has touched this stuff since it was unloaded off the Mayflower.

"Wait!" I flap my hands to slice through the dust. "There's something back there."

Behind the boxes, lined up like soldiers, I see them. I cough some dust, squeeze past the boxes, and reach out to grab what may be treasure.

"Look, old canvases!" I pull some out, one at a time. A landscape of city buildings. A still life of flowers. A portrait of a man with a pipe and captain's hat. Even though the colors are dark and muddy from layers of dirt, the paintings are really neat in an old-fashioned kind of way.

Bill steps past me to get a better look. He flips through the paintings and quickly pulls one out.

"Wow!" His mouth drops open and he turns the painting towards me.

I feel my face turn beet red. In the painting, I see flesh. Womanly flesh. Arms and legs and belly and, yep, more. Right in front of my eyes. And in front of Bill's eyes, which have opened so wide, they almost pop out of their sockets.

"Look at these!" Bill pulls out more canvases.

More flesh. All colors of flesh. All sizes of flesh. All shapes of flesh. Men. Women.

I can't not look. What's the big deal anyway? Museums are filled with lots of naked people. I mean, lots of paintings of naked people. And statues.

In this tight garage, Bill and I are looking at same nakedness together, so I'm as embarrassed as if I'm standing here naked myself. But Bill is so enthralled with the paintings, I doubt he even remembers I'm here.

My curiosity makes me keep looking.

"Who painted these?" I see initials in the corner of one painting. "M.M. Who's M.M?"

"I don't know," Bill says. "But I would like to meet him and shake his hand. These are gorgeous."

I slug his arm. "You mean the paintings or the models? You're such a pig."

While Bill ogles some more, I spot a glint of something metallic tucked into the wood framing of the garage. I pull out a large, tarnished medal and rub my hand over the surface.

"Look at this. 'Presented to Margherita Morandi for Excellence in Art. 1941.' That must be who M.M. is." I try to hand the medal to Bill, but his eyes are still glued to the paintings.

"Yes, he sure did excellent work," Bill grins.

"You dope. Margherita is not a man's name. So you think a woman did excellent work?"

"Umm..." He's speechless for a change.

Mrs. Egan calls from the house. "Remmy? Bill? What's taking so long?"

"Quick." I put the medal back. "Put everything away." Bill starts to protest, but I say, "These paintings are none of our business."

We restack the paintings, drag boxes back into place, and head into the house.

Mrs. Egan has set up a still life of pots and pitchers—white ceramic, dented copper, pewter, vegetable-patterned pottery, cut crystal. Painting all the different surfaces and textures will be a huge challenge. But first things first.

"Mrs. Egan, we couldn't find a place to squeeze in the easel, so we left it outside the garage," I say. Some garage dust tickles my nose and I sneeze. A tiny giggle escapes my mouth.

"Oh, that's what I feared. One of these mornings, my poor husband will be ready to leave for work and his car will have been swallowed up in that hodgepodge. I'll see if he can rearrange things tomorrow to accommodate the easel. Or maybe we should just use it for kindling."

She laughs and pats me on the back. "Just carrying the easel down for me was a great help, my darling fledglings. Now that we've got a bit more elbow room, we can even dance." She wiggles her hips and swings her arms around to confirm that, and then turns to tinker with the composition of the pots.

Bill and I look at each other and share a secret smile. I see a glimpse of the Bill I used to know—that sparkle in his eyes.

17 • April Alone

April has brought the return of spring, but not the return of my friendship with Debbie. There's a big hole in my heart and I've had to accept that years of friendship don't guarantee a friendship will last forever. Mom says it's part of growing up and sometimes people grow in different directions and usually it's for the best. But right now it doesn't feel it's for the best.

Although Debbie and I have moved in different directions, it's awkward when those directions collide. Like today.

* * * * *

After school, the athletic field swarms with boys swinging bats and throwing balls, thrilled to finally escape the prison of winter. I stop next to a tree to watch the baseball activity through a chain link fence. I used to play ball with some of the same boys in the neighborhood, but in junior high, baseball is just for boys.

Above the racket on the field, I hear a loud cackle and realize Debbie and The Rat Fink are also watching the action from the far end of the fence. I quickly slip behind the tree. I bet they're trying to pick out Jacques in all the running and bobbing boys. I wonder if Debbie has made any progress with her resolution, but I doubt it.

"Boys love it when girls watch them play," I hear Debbie say to The Rat Fink. "It makes them feel powerful when they have our admiration."

I'd rather be playing than admiring.

There's a squeal and Debbie's arm shoots out and points. "I see him! Over there. In the blue cap. Ah, I can feel his Frenchness from here."

Oh brother.

My attention drifts away from the ball players and I notice spring buds dotting the branches of the trees lining the field. Last fall, gold, orange, and red leaves looked like a colorful scarf trying to keep the same trees warm. That would make an award-winning painting. But the Art Awards are only two months away and there's no time to wait to paint the turning leaves.

More squeals come from the other end of the fence. I'd better leave before the cackling friends spot me.

"Hi, Miss Rembrandt."

I duck back behind the tree.

Bill walks my way. His bangs sweep across his eyebrows.

"Checking out the talent?" he asks.

"Um, not really."

Bill leans on the fence. "I think I see dreamy Peter out there."

A hot flush travels up my neck. I need to shift this conversation.

"Why aren't you out there showing off with your baseball buddies?" I ask him.

"Um, I have a doctor's appointment." He looks out at the field. "I've got plenty of time to toss the ball around with the guys before Little League tryouts."

Sure. And I have plenty of time to fly to Mars and back.

There's a crack of a bat and yells of "Heads up!" We crouch and cover our heads as a ball flies over the fence, and bounces on the ground just past us.

"A little help?" Hazeliscious Peter runs towards us, waving his glove, and I'm trapped in the spell. It takes me a second to realize what he said since I'm staring at his eyes.

"Oh. I'll get it," I say since Bill doesn't budge. I trot over to the ball and hurl it back over the fence. It makes a satisfying thunk into Peter's glove.

His hazeliscious eyes widen in surprise. "Thanks, Remmy!" he yells. "You've got a great arm."

I know I do and proudly lift my chin. Peter complimented me and the world is singing!

"Come to Little League tryouts, and make sure you wear a pretty dress and hair bows!" he laughs.

The guys with Peter howl and snicker as they head back to practice.

Debbie and The Rat Fink spot me and are laughing, too, and then whispering.

I quickly turn to run away and forget that Bill is standing right in front of me and we collide in a clumsy way that doesn't knock us down but we end up holding each other. We shake each other off and mutter "Sorry."

My former friend laughs again and scurries away with The Rat Fink.

"Wow, Miss Rembrandt! You do have a great arm." Bill's eyes get huge and he's acting like a little kid who just bumped into Whitey Ford. "Where did that come from?"

I know exactly where that came from.

"My father used to play catch with me." Big deal. Dad quit playing when he realized it was pointless to train a girl.

Bill studies my face for an uncomfortable amount of time. Is there a zit forming on the tip of my chin? Is there spinach in my teeth even though I don't eat spinach? Is something hanging out of my nose? I brace myself for one of his typical insults.

Instead, he takes off.

What was that about?

I turn back to the fence and watch the boys scrambling around the field.

It feels like I'm looking through prison bars.

18 • The Deal With Bill

The next morning, in my locker, I find a note written in rushed, wriggly handwriting. "Meet me in the art room after school. Bill."

Why? He was so strange at the field yesterday with those stares and those questions like he never saw a girl throw a baseball before. What is he up to? This could be some kind of ambush, like maybe he has an evil plan to get me out of the art contest or maybe he's so threatened by my talent he wants to destroy my fingers. Well, there's only one way to find out. When the three o'clock bell rings, I courageously head to the art room.

Bill is sitting at one of the desks, head down, long bangs covering his eyes, and drawing intently on a piece of newsprint paper. There's a desk pulled up next to his with more paper and pencils.

"What do you want?" I stand at the door, keeping my distance, on the watch for any outward sign of attack.

Bill looks up and motions with his hand. "Remmy, sit here. Quickly."

Remmy? When has he ever called me Remmy?

When I don't move, he attempts a crooked smile. "C'mon, sit down. What's your problem?"

I slowly walk over and slide into the seat next to him. His paper is covered with random squiggles and scratches. Okay, it's official. He's crazy.

"Just pretend you're drawing." He keeps scribbling and glancing at the door.

I pick up a blue pencil. "What's going on?"

"Draw!" he says in a whispered yell.

I scribble.

His whispering continues. "I don't want anyone to suspect anything, especially those jocks."

"Those jocks? You mean your dumb pack of goofballs?" I whisper back. "And what are we doing that's so suspicious, anyway?"

We both keep our heads down, suspiciously scribbling.

"I need your help," Bill says. "But it has to be a complete secret. No one can know about this."

Now he's gotten my attention. I hope this has nothing to do with those naked paintings in Mrs. Egan's garage. That's the only secret I can think of we have together. And he would never admit to needing any help with art. Maybe math homework? Or the *Great Gatsby* book report due next week?

Bill gives the door another quick look and goes back to scribbling.

"That was a pretty amazing throw you made yesterday," he says.

"Even for a girl?"

"Especially for a girl."

It's amazing how Bill can turn a compliment into an insult so quickly. If he keeps talking like this, I'll turn him down faster than the speed of light.

"Look, if I want to stay in good with the guys, I have to try out for Little League." He keeps his eyes glued to his paper, but a blush creeps up his neck. "I want you to help me practice baseball. I really need practice. I mean, really. A lot!"

"Well, why don't you ask one of your precious jocks for help?" If he thinks boys are so superior, then let him get help from them.

He brushes his bangs away from his eyes, and looks around at the artwork on the walls. He taps his pencil on the desk, and scrunches his lips together, like he needs to let out more words but wants to hold them in at the same time.

I wait.

His eyes fix on a drawing of his tacked to the bulletin board.

"I'm an artist, Remmy. Not a ballplayer."

"Oh, there's a news flash. Call Walter Cronkite." I laugh.

Bill slams down his pencil. "This isn't funny. Do you know what those baseball guys or basketball guys or football guys think of art?"

I can guess, but I don't say.

"It's sissy stuff," he says, still not looking at me. He takes a deep breath and pushes out the words, "They don't think much of sissies."

"Sissy stuff? What about all your famous manly artists in history?" I can't stop myself from rubbing it in after all the grief and teasing he's given me. "Especially your main manly man Picasso?"

He finally looks me in the eye. "If a guy is a good athlete, like Peter, he can get away with being an artist. If not, then he's a sissy. That's the way it is."

So boys have Rules, too, and that's the way it is?

"Please, Remmy. Help me." Bill's eyes are edged with red.

Wow, this is serious. Like really serious. I start to sympathize with him, but quickly pull myself together, replaying in my mind all the insults he's ever thrown at me.

"Well, why should I help you? We used to help each other a lot, remember?" I ask.

"Sure I remember," Bill smiles. "But that was in the old days."

"The old days? We only left elementary school last year." Do boys have any sense of time or do they just have their own messed-up inner calendar?

"Please, Remmy?" Bill asks again.

As much as I hate all his usual showing off and arrogance, this begging is even worse, and he looks so pitiful and hurting. But some not-so-nice part of me is enjoying watching him squirm.

"Well, what do I get out of this?" He's going to have to do some serious convincing before I agree to help him.

He thinks. "Um, I promise to not tease you anymore?"

I don't budge. I've had to harden my shell against his teases, so that's no big deal. I shake my head no.

"And I'll buy you the *Beatles '65* album."

"Got it already." How can he not remember what a devoted Beatlemaniac I am?

"How about *The Early Beatles*? Woolworth's just put the new album out yesterday."

Holy John-Paul-George-and-Ringo! It's out already? I have to get that album! But even though I'm softening, I bite my lip and keep on my poker face.

"Look." He pulls a crumpled five-dollar bill from his pocket. "I just got this birthday money from my grandma." He looks at it, hesitates, and takes a deep breath. "It's yours, if you help me."

He holds the bill out to me and I grab the money.

"Plus the album and you've got a deal!"

I shoot out my hand to seal the deal and he gently shakes it and a wave of relief spreads across his face. Then he grabs his pencil again, looks down smiling, and starts scribbling. I do, too.

Wait. All this scribbling is ridiculous and I put the pencil down. The deal has been done so why am I still hanging around?

When I stand, Bill says, "You'd better leave by yourself, so no one sees us together."

At the doorway, I turn back to give him a warm, comforting smile to let him know things will be okay. But his head is down and his hand is still scribbling. He doesn't see my smile.

19 • Spring Training

Little kids scream and chase each other around the concrete playground and swing on swings while Bill and I hide near the grass field in the shadow of Our Lady of Mt. Carmel Elementary School. Nobody we know from Ben Franklin ever plays in this field. Hopefully.

Bill's baseball cap is pulled way down to his ears with his hair tucked up inside. He's wearing dark sunglasses and a jumbo black and orange t-shirt that says "Princeton." If ball players were spies, Bill is dressing the part.

"Maybe you should have worn a fake moustache, too," I say.

If he's glaring at me, I can't tell because of the sunglasses, although his body language suggests that he is.

We scan the playground again before stepping out into the sun and heading to the far corner of the empty field away from all the kids. My old glove is tight and stiff from lack of use, but it will do.

"Okay, throw me the ball." I pound the pocket of my glove and wait.

Bill pulls back his arm and flips it forward like a wriggling fish. The ball arches high and drops to the ground two feet in front of me.

"Well, that's a start." I trot forward, pick up the ball, and zip it back to him. He ducks and covers his head with his glove.

"What are you doing? Catch the ball!" I yell.

"I wasn't ready." He retrieves the ball and sends it back to me, but it flies way over my head and into the bushes.

We try a couple of lame volleys back and forth, but every time I'm about to throw him the ball, Bill's looking around in the other direction.

"Hey!" I call to him and wave my glove. "You know, there's an expression: 'Keep your eye on the ball.' Ever heard that?"

"Yeah, yeah. I just don't want to get caught with you." He looks around again even though the kids running around the playground are at least a foot shorter than us and don't resemble any seventh grader I know.

"If you keep spinning around like a lawn sprinkler, you'll never get any practice."

"Okay. You're right." Bill aims his head and body directly at me.

It doesn't help. He still misses the ball. Over and over. I change strategies and decide we should switch to distance throwing.

"Back up," I shout. "We'll pretend you're out in left field and

you want to pick off a player at second. I'm the second baseman."

I wave him back and back up myself so there's as much space between us as possible. Bill looks at me (I think. He's still wearing the sunglasses) with his lips pressed together in determination. He heaves the ball and it soars way too high and far. The ball reaches the top of a high arch and seems to hover in space before starting its descent. I track it with my eyes and back up, my glove high, anticipating where the ball might land. I pick up speed running backwards and at the same time I sense another moving object coming towards me, but I don't take my eye off the ball.

Thunk! The ball snaps into my glove. But then a powerful force tackles me and rolls with me and rolls with me until the rolling stops behind a bush. A big sweaty weight is on top of me.

"WHAT THE...?"

Bill quickly jumps off me but covers my mouth with his sweaty hand and muffles my words.

"SSSSSSsssssssh!" he shushes. I wriggle, trying to get loose of his hold, but give up. His eyes get large and he holds his breath. We're very quiet.

Then I hear it. A loud, evil cackle.

The Rat Fink!

Bill and I carefully peek from behind the bush. The Rat Fink's yelling at her little brother that it's time to go home and look at what a mess he is and stop dragging his feet. The two of them leave the playground, and she yanks her brother down the street. She stops and, with a frown, looks back for a minute. Then, she gives her brother a shove and they leave.

"That was close," I whisper.

Bill's face is white and he says nothing.

* * * * *

For our next practices, Bill and I ride our bikes separately to a ball field in the next town over. I'd love to say that Bill miraculously turns into Mickey Mantle under my coaching. But he's still more like Mickey Mouse.

"Bill," I look into his dark lenses. "Are you sure you want to keep going?"

"No, I'm not sure." He straightens up and throws back his shoulders. "But I have to."

"Why do you care what those jocks think?"

He's silent.

"Pablo Picasso doesn't care what anyone else thinks. Only his art matters." I hope his idol can knock some sense into him. "And women are crazy for him." Which I don't get. "I bet he didn't have to show off in sports when he was a kid."

"Picasso didn't go to Ben Franklin Junior High when he was twelve."

True.

I punch the pocket of my glove. "Okay. Let's get back to work," I say.

Bill nods. "Thanks, Remmy."

20 • Strike Out

The day is here. It's time for my coaching skills to be put to the test.

Clusters of girls rim the ball field, while boys in caps and sneakers line up in front of a row of tables. Bill made me swear that I'd be here for Little League tryouts, but I can't find him in any of the sign-up lines or on the field.

"Remmy! What are you doing here?"

I turn and meet Peter's big hazeliscious eyes. My knees instantly wobble and I struggle to spit out a reply.

"Oh! I'm looking for Bill." But I only look at Peter. "He's trying out."

My search for Bill freezes as I fall under Peter's spell, but then I get worried that my star pupil still hasn't shown up.

Peter moves to one of the registration lines. I look for Bill again, but then follow Peter and stand in line with him, grinning stupidly. I'm almost ready to forget he laughed at me. Almost.

But still, where's Bill? He wants this so much and worked so hard.

"Look, here he comes." Peter points to a figure limping towards us on crutches.

Holy Mickey Mantle! Bill chickened out.

"What happened?" Peter asks.

"Boy, the worst luck!" Bill won't look at me. "I was helping my stupid brother work on his motorcycle and the bozo knocked it over, which knocked me over. My ankle's only sprained, but I'll be on crutches for two weeks."

"Aw, that stinks." Peter's eyebrows frown over those eyes.

He believes this pathetic lie? I frown at Bill too for a different reason, but he still won't look at me.

The three of us inch forward in the line until it's Peter's turn to register. When he steps up to the table, I poke Bill.

"You idiot! All that practice!" I whisper-hiss at Bill. "And now you're using those crutches for two weeks just to fink out?"

"Well, it's better than making a fool of myself on that field." He looks down at his bandaged foot.

"You should have realized that before you roped me into your stupid plan. You're hopeless." All that time wasted when I could have been drawing or painting or doing just about anything else.

"But I had to try." He looks pathetic.

"Well, don't even think about getting that album or your money back!"

"It doesn't matter. I wasn't getting my money's worth anyway!"

Our angry whispering sounds like a swarm of hornets and the boys behind us in line are starting to notice. But I don't care. I'm burning mad.

"You should just admit it. YOU ARE A SISSY!" I blurt out at full volume.

I slap my hands across my mouth. Oh no. I want to suck those words right back into my mouth.

The boys behind us in line laugh and nudge each other.

Bill bares his teeth at me, like a hurt, angry, stray dog. How could I say that? I start to apologize, but Bill clomps off quickly on his crutches towards the field exit and I don't try to stop him.

When I turn back, I see that Peter is still registering and missed all the drama. Phew.

When he finishes, Peter steps to the side and there's nothing between me and the registration table. Drops of sweat dot the bald head of the man at the table, his eyes down as he scribbles on his clipboard.

"NEXT! Name, please." He doesn't look up.

I freeze. I don't belong here. But I take a step forward anyway.

"Name, please!" Baldy yells again.

"Rosella Rinaldi."

The man's face shoots up and wrinkles like a bulldog. "That's an odd name for a boy!" he barks.

"I agree. But I'm not a boy. And actually most people call me Remmy and I..."

"Stop!" Baldy taps his pen against the clipboard. "Why are you here?"

"I...I..." I see Peter grinning and nodding his head. "I thought I'd sign up for Little League. I'm a really good player." Especially after all that time spent training Bill.

There's silence at the table and snickers behind me in line.

"She actually has a great arm, Coach."

I smile at Peter. He's redeemed himself.

"Who are you? Her agent?" Baldy snarls at Peter. Then he looks back at me. "I don't care what kind of arm you have, missy. It's a girl's arm. No girls!" He waves me away. "Those are the rules. That's the way it's always been. And that's the way it always *will* be. No girls!"

He can't be right, just like Bill can't be right about women artists. It's not fair.

"But if you just let me tryout..."

"Case closed! You're wasting my time. Move along."

He starts to stand and I back away from the table. I hear laughing and hooting all around me. Seeing a baseball on the table, I grab it and hurl it as hard as I can over the heads of the boys still on line. As they turn to watch the ball clear the pitcher's mound of the nearby diamond, I run away in the opposite direction, not slowing down until the laughter from the field fades away from my ears.

At home, I stomp down to the playroom, flick on the TV, and curl into a ball in Dad's chair. *You're wasting my time. Move along. That's the way it always will be.* The coach's words loop over and over in my head. I hadn't even planned to try out. Why am I so angry? Because it's not fair, that's why.

I stay curled up for hours, staring at the TV in a furious fog. Couples dance in tuxedos and long gowns, cops chase gangsters, cowboys sing, and they all blur together in black and white like one long meaningless movie.

"What are you watching there?" Dad approaches his chair and looks at the screen.

I sit up and try to focus. "Um...*Million Dollar Movie*?"

Dad playfully taps me on the head with his newspaper. "Since when do you like old movies?"

I shrug my shoulders. Since life isn't fair?

"May I have my chair? The Yankees game is starting soon." Dad takes the seat I had warmed up. "Want to watch?"

"No, I don't want to watch! I hate baseball!" I race to my room before he can react.

In my room, I can't get the baseball field out of my head. I see Bill's face when I called him a sissy and my stomach turns. He didn't deserve that. Why is Bill forced to be an athlete and I'm not allowed to be? There are so many unfair rules.

I look at the WOW!Wall and see the Beatles grinning out at me from a tacked-up magazine page.

"I bet you lads had rules to put up with, too. You broke rules with those haircuts and your music breaks rules and just look how famous you are!"

Well, maybe I'm ready to break some rules too.

A plan forms in my head that makes so much sense, I wish I

had thought of it sooner. The girls at school will be so thrilled by their new freedom, I'll be a hero! I get a shopping bag and open the bottom drawer of my dresser.

The Beatles sing in my head "because I told you before, oh, you can't do that..."

Wanna bet? Just watch.

21 • Taking A Stand

The next morning at school, I slip into the girls room and empty the shopping bag. Butterflies in my stomach are doing dive bombs as I get ready, but I'm totally committed to my plan. I step out of my skirt and complete my transformation.

Okay. It's show time!

I peek out the girls room door, take a deep breath, and step out into the hallway. I look down, admire my outfit, and do a little tap dance. This feels great! Dungarees and Keds. The soft denim pants warm my legs and the sneakers snuggle my toes. I'm tired of wearing dresses and skirts to school and to the supermarket and to the movies and to just about everywhere else.

Head held high and a smile on my face, I strut down the hallway towards my homeroom. A group of ninth-grade girls sends me icy stares of disapproval as they slink by.

Then I spot an army of one marching towards me. The Rat Fink.

"Hey, Ellie May, are you gonna be sloppin' some hogs?" she yells when she spots me. Other kids turn and laugh when they see me.

"Hee haw, Old McDonald!" another voice shouts from the gathering crowd. Kids are pointing and craning their necks and pushing in to get a look.

I meet all their eyes. "It's not fair that we girls are trapped in skirts and all kinds of other restrictions." I cross my arms and plant myself firmly in my Keds, prepared for battle. "I'm taking a stand."

With so many eyes on me, it's time to rally. I see that Debbie is now standing next to The Rat Fink, her mouth hanging open. My legs wobble a bit, but I get ahold of myself.

"Yes, I'm breaking the rules!" I say loudly. "Why can't I be comfortable? It's my right. And the right of all you girls. Are you with me?" I raise my arms.

There has to be at least one uncomfortable girl—another rebel—in this crowd. But no one raises a hand. No one cheers "Yeah!" No one even nods in agreement.

"And is it your right to be in Little League, too?" The Rat Fink nudges Debbie, who looks back at her, puzzled. "Oh, didn't you hear? Remmy tried to sign up for Little League yesterday."

I glare at The Rat Fink and my confidence dips. "Well, it was kind of an accident," I try to explain. "You see, I was trying to help Bill and then Peter was on line and then I was at the head of the line and Baldy said..."

132

"You really are nuts!" Debbie yells.

Of course she isn't backing me up.

But maybe I've made a huge mistake. Am I the only girl in the world who doesn't want to follow the rules that girls are stuck with?

The Rat Fink butts in. "Before you know it, Remmy will want to be a fireman carrying people out of burning buildings or a policeman chasing the bad guys."

When she hears laughter from the crowd, The Rat Fink keeps going and plays to her audience. "Or how about an astronaut? Yeah, Remmy flies to Moon!"

She won't stop.

"Oh, I know. Why don't you become a soldier, Remmy, and go fight in a war? Get yourself a gun, jump in a fox hole, and save America from Communism. It's your right."

The crowd laughs even louder.

"Why not? I can be anything I want." My heart feels it's true, but my brain worries that the world's rules are stronger than me. It's difficult for a girl to become a fireman or policeman or astronaut. Or even a great artist? It's not fair!

Debbie pushes her way out of the crowd and disappears as Principal Schlafly comes barreling down the hall, cutting through kids like a football player. "What's all this ruckus?"

"Nothing, Principal Schlafly," says The Rat Fink. "I think Remmy is a little confused about proper school clothing. Or maybe her legs are just cold." Having made her point, she scurries down the hall to her classroom.

The principal's eyes pop when he sees what I'm wearing. I feel more naked than those mysterious paintings in Mrs. Egan's garage.

"All right." Principal Schlafly stares down every kid in the hall. "Get to your classrooms, now! The sideshow is over."

Kids scramble in every direction and disappear.

I sprint towards the girls room, but the principal barks, "Miss Rinaldi! My office. Now."

My Keds squeak like mice as I follow Principal Schlafly down the deserted hallway. Passing a classroom, I see Bill standing in the doorway with his crutches and fake sprain. He must have heard the whole commotion. I feel so awful about yesterday. When I mouth to him "I'm sorry," he turns away and hobbles into the classroom.

I squirm in the principal's office chair. I haven't spent much time in this office and the dungarees are not helping my comfort level right now. They're making me swelter. Or am I making me swelter?

"Miss Rinaldi, we have rules in this school so that we can properly educate young men and young women. What would happen if all the rules were thrown out?" Principal Schlafly squints at me though his black-rimmed glasses.

I look down at my hands. I'd be a happier person?

"There would be chaos, confusion...even anarchy!" he answers for me.

I'm not even sure what anarchy means but it sounds very serious.

"I don't see how girls wearing pants to school would cause

134

chaos." Talking back to an adult feels uncomfortable but strangely satisfying at the same time. Principal Schlafly's eyebrows shoot up.

"It is indecent behavior," he blusters. "Girls and boys must live within their roles...I mean, the rules."

Principal Schlafly thinks a minute. "Miss Rinaldi, I consider you a reasonable and well-behaved young lady. This little demonstration of yours is quite out of character." He stands. "But if anything like this happens again, you will be disciplined. I don't want to hear any more nonsense about your inappropriate choice of wardrobe. Change back into proper clothing and go to your next class. The secretary will give you a pass."

I take the pass and carry my shopping bag into the girls room to change. Back in my skirt and loafers, I look at myself in the mirror. I'm back to being "proper." I can't be the only one who feels things are unfair. Is it "nonsense" for a girl to want to be equal? All I know is that I'm not ready to give up this nonsense. When I win the Art Awards contest, everyone will see that a girl can be the best.

This girl.

22 • Getting Closer

The artist in me loves seeing new flowers blooming during this new month of May with all the splashes of colors like nature's own paint palette. Pages in my Super Secret Sketchbook have turned into gardens and bouquets inspired by van Gogh and Monet. And painting at Mrs. Egan's every week adds another contender for my award-winning portfolio.

And best of all, I'm no longer disturbed by the friendship between Debbie and The Rat Fink. They deserve each other. It's just been me and My Spark and it's a perfect partnership.

* * * * *

Standing at my easel in Mrs. Egan's studio, I look from the arrangement of dogwood branches in a cut-crystal vase, then back to my painting and add more highlights on the vase. If I had tried to paint this vase back in January, it would have looked like a metal army canteen. I've really made progress. Unfortunately, this is our last lesson until the fall.

"That's not bad, Miss Rembrandt." Bill stands behind me, getting ready to clean off his brushes. "Although not spectacular enough to beat me in the Art Awards contest."

I glare at him and whisper, "What happened to our deal? You know, no teasing?"

"Oh, I'm not teasing. I'm stating a fact," he says coldly.

I wish I could turn back time and erase my hurtful words at the Little League tryouts. Whenever I try to apologize to Bill, the words gag in my throat and I turn away from him.

Peter quit the lessons because his baseball team made it to the semifinals and he's busy with practice. I haven't had those hazeliscious eyes distracting me, so it's easier to concentrate on my work without having to pretend he isn't in the room when he actually is.

Karen hums, oblivious to the discussion. Her painting is unfinished. The flowers and branches look like flowers and branches, but the vase is still just a flat gray shape. She enjoys coming here, but it's not her Spark like it is mine.

"Did you decide yet if you're entering the Art Awards?" I ask her.

"I'm not going to. I'm just too busy practicing for the spring concert. If I do really well, I'll move up to second violin chair next to Tommy Clementi." Karen pushes back her red curls,

138

frowns at her painting, and shrugs her shoulders. She resumes humming something that sounds classical and fingers the neck of her brush. Her mind has left her canvas and is back with her violin.

While Bill is busy cleaning his palette and brushes, I sneak a long look at his painting. Curses! It's great. The dogwood blossoms are softly-blushing pink and are translucent against the knobby branches. The crystal vase sparkles with tiny rainbows of reflections. He even indicated the embroidery on the tablecloth. His painting makes my stomach hurt it's so good. I hop back to my easel before he notices me.

"I'm coming, my darlings!" There are footsteps on the stairs, the jangle of bangles, and Mrs. Egan returns to the attic.

"I'm so sorry I took so long. I have a little gift for each of you and couldn't remember where I put them." She taps the top of her head. "This noggin ain't what it used to be. Then I remembered I left the gifts in a bag in the garage."

The garage. Bill and I exchange a secret smile, remembering our discovery out there. I feel myself blush, thinking about those paintings, and I quickly look away from him. Maybe his anger is starting to dissolve after all.

"Don't let your drawing skills get rusty this summer." Mrs. Egan hands each of us a sketchbook with a brown leatherette cover. I gently run my hand across it as if it holds precious sketches by Leonardo himself.

"Just like tennis players need to practice their serves, artists need to practice their craft. Your drawing skills are like muscles that must be used continuously so they get stronger and finer." She flexes her arms to demonstrate her point and laughs. "Draw whatever your hearts' desire and bring your sketchbook back in the fall so I can see what inspired you."

Bill and Karen bundle up their supplies and final painting. They say their thanks and goodbyes, and tromp down the stairs, but I linger behind.

"Mrs. Egan, may I ask you a favor?" I sure hopes she buys this.

"Of course, dear. How can I help?"

I look at her Capri pants, striped shirt, and big chartreuse bangle earrings.

"Um, do you own a suit?" I ask.

"Why? Am I dressing too avant-garde for our lessons? Should I look more professorial?" Her face is serious, but then she breaks in a big smile and winks.

"Oh, no, no, no." I quickly explain. "I want you to pose for me. For a portrait. In a suit."

She hesitates and I know I've come up with a super dumb idea.

"Is a red suit okay?" she asks.

Of course she wouldn't have just an ordinary brown or gray suit.

"That's perfect." Red is the color of power.

"I'm speculating that this portrait must be for your Art Awards portfolio." She makes a deep curtsy. "I am truly honored, Miss Rinaldi."

"Oh, it's not just a portrait. It's my Vision of the Year 2000.

It'll be a statement. Maybe even a manifesto!" When I tell her my secret concept, her broad grin gives me all the encouragement I need. We schedule our first sitting for Tuesday and I know I'll paint a winner.

23 • Painting the Vision

Tuesday can't come soon enough and I race to Mrs. Egan's right after school. She already has her suit on, with her hair swept up into a French twist. Very elegant. Like Jackie Kennedy or Audrey Hepburn.

In the attic, she's hung a white sheet and placed a stool in front of it because I told her about the background I was going to add later.

After I set up my palette and easel, Mrs. Egan perches on the stool.

"Should I face directly at you? Or maybe a three-quarters pose?"

She swivels front and side and front and side, trying to help me make a decision. Then it hits me. I'm about to paint my teacher—someone I admire and trust.

"Remmy? What do you think?" Mrs. Egan is waiting.

What do I think? Debbie's angry words barge in and make me freeze: *How could you do this to me?! You are so mean and you're a terrible artist and you'll never win that stupid contest!* The one time I attempted a portrait I killed a friendship.

Mrs. Egan gets off the stool. "You look pale. Are you okay?"

"I don't know if I can do this."

"Of course you can do this. Look at how much progress you've made in this class," she says. "This is just a new kind of challenge. Think of me as a large bowl of fruit."

I laugh.

"Seriously. You know how to show volumes with lines and shadows and highlights. A portrait is the same. A face is all lines, shadows and highlights. Apples have skin. I have skin. A tablecloth has wrinkles. I have wrinkles." Mrs. Egan chuckles. "And, as I've told you, you have an instinctive sense of color."

And inherited, I think.

"Okay. Let's go with the three-quarter pose." I pick up my brush.

Mrs. Egan hops back on the stool and takes the pose. "You've got this, Remmy."

I nod. She looks like a woman of decision. Just like my Vision of the Year 2000. The concept of my Vision gives me confidence and I get to work.

After about 15 minutes, Mrs. Egan wiggles her shoulders and says, "I need to take a break before my fingers get numb and fall off. Not to mention my derrière. Actually, I wouldn't mind losing a little derrière." She laughs, stands, and stretches.

She comes around to look at my canvas. "You're off to a great start with the underdrawing. Just double check the position of the left eye in relationship to the tip of the nose. It looks a little off. Maybe too low." She squints at my painting and tilts her head. "Here's a great trick to see if anything is out of place."

She turns my canvas upside down and we both step back to look. The under drawing is no longer a person, but a composition of elements so it's easier to see if something is wrong.

"Yeah, I see what you mean about that eye." Since the drawing is painted with a mixture of burnt sienna and ultramarine blue thinned with linseed oil, it's easy to erase with some turpentine on a cloth and fix .

I turn the canvas right-side up and sigh. I want so much to win and prove to Dad and Bill that they are wrong about me.

"You know, Bill says there aren't any great women artists," I say. "He thinks men run everything."

I wait for her reaction, knowing he's totally wrong.

"That boy..." she sighs. "I hate to say it but he's partially right."

Holy Mona Lisa!

"It *is* a man's world. Men have more opportunities. They have the jobs of power and money. They are the heads of the family."

I don't want to hear this even though I know it's the truth. I see how Mom defers to Dad.

Mrs. Egan pats my shoulder. "Trust me, Remmy. There are accomplished female artists."

"Then why are there no women artists in my *History of Art* book? I mean, in all 572 pages and 17,000 years? No women?"

She shakes her head. "Yes, I know that book and so does every college art student. I suppose the author, Professor Janson, has the same attitudes as Bill and didn't look deeply enough for the women hidden behind more famous men."

I toss down my brush. "So if women are hidden, why am I wasting my time with this?"

I think about playing catch with my father and how that led to nothing. Is he right about me becoming a valuable secretary instead of a hidden artist? Typewriters instead of brushes?

"Remmy, you're not wasting your time." She gives me a worried look. "Women just need to work harder to achieve success, but it's not impossible. We have more barriers to break through. We need to persist and do the best work we possibly can. Then someday, women will step out of the shadows."

Someday. How far away is someday?

"Wait. I'll show you something." Mrs. Egan goes to the bookshelf, runs her finger along the spines, and pulls out a booklet. "Good. I found it."

She hands it to me. "I saw this fascinating museum exhibit in Massachusetts a few years ago."

"Worchester Museum. 1960. Miss Georgia O'Keeffe," I read. The black and white pages have paintings of city buildings, mountains, animal skulls, and huge flowers that fill entire canvases.

"You should see these paintings in color! Miss O'Keeffe is a

146

spectacular artist. Look at the strength and uniqueness of each one." Mrs. Egan's eyes light up like I've never seen.

Miss O'Keeffe is an awesome artist but she isn't in my art history book.

"And have you seen Mary Cassatt's paintings at the Metropolitan Museum of Art?" Mrs. Egan asks. "Her paintings of mothers and children are so special." When I shake my head no, she says, "I must take you. Maybe in the fall, I'll take our whole group. Yes, yes, that's what we'll do. We'll show Bill what women can achieve."

I look back through the gallery catalog. I feel like Archimedes in the bathtub. Eureka! I have found her! An amazing woman artist. And another at the Met. And there must be more.

Mrs. Egan takes her place on the stool and looks right at me as I dip a rag into turpentine and erase the off-balance eye from my underdrawing. I notice a glint of tear in her eye.

24 • The Truth Comes Out

A t our third portrait session, Mrs. Egan tilts her head and takes a long look at my painting. I realize I'm holding my breath as I wait for a verdict.

"This is quite lovely, dear. I mean your painting, not my face." She laughs and I start to breath again.

"Here's a tip. If you add a bit of green to the shadow, the pink in the cheek will look pinker. Anytime you want to bring out a color, put its complimentary color next to it. Like purple next to yellow, orange next to blue."

Mrs. Egan takes her place back on the stool and I get to work. The green in the shadow really does make the pink of the cheek stand out, like she said it would.

I work on adding detail to her eyes, trying to capture her look of termination. I should be able to finish the portrait today and my Vision of the Year 2000 will be ready to impress everyone at the Art Awards in a couple of weeks.

As I turn towards my palette, a print of a Gauguin painting on the wall catches my eye, especially the lack of clothing on the women. I feel myself blush and quickly look away, but it makes me remember that secret out in the garage.

If I don't ask Mrs. Egan about those paintings now, while we're alone, I may never have the chance. But talking about naked paintings is embarrassing. The modest me is fighting with the curious me, but one of them wins.

"Who is M. M.?" I ask.

"What?"

"M. M.?"

Mrs. Egan's face goes pale.

"We didn't mean to be nosy, but Bill and I found some paintings in your garage. They are...um...interesting." I can still see all that flesh.

"M. M. is Margherita Morandi," she says slowly.

Well, I already know that from the medal. "But who *is* she? Really?"

Mrs. Egan squirms on the stool and says something in a low voice.

"Who?" I ask again.

"She is me!" she says, standing. "I am the talented Margherita Morandi."

"You are? But..."

"That was my name before I married. Margherita is Italian

for Margaret. And a nickname for Margaret is Peggy. So here I am. Peggy Egan, alias Margherita Morandi."

"So you did those paintings? All of them? Even the, the..."

"The nudes?" she laughs. "Yes, even the nudes."

"And the medal?"

"Ah, so you also found the medal."

"I'm sorry, but the medal looked so impressive I can't forget it."

Mrs. Egan takes a deep breath. "Yes, it was impressive at the time. The most important thing that had ever happened to me. I won an art school scholarship at the end of high school."

"Wow!"

"Yes, wow. But, America had just entered World War II and my brother was drafted into the Army. My father needed me to take my brother's place in our pizzeria and wouldn't let me take the scholarship."

She stops and brushes at her jacket, not looking at me. "There was no other choice, but it broke my heart."

I've never seen her look sad.

She walks to the window, looking out with her back to me.

Why did I bring up these memories for her? I saw all that talent in the garage and was curious, but now I've hurt her.

"That was such a long time ago," I say. "Things have changed." Although, thinking about my own father's attitude, maybe things haven't changed all that much.

"Why aren't you still painting?" How can she ignore her talent?

Mrs. Egan turns away from the window to face me. Her eyes are red. She makes a crooked smile.

"Well, I went to painting classes for a few years at the Art Students League on my day off from the restaurant. And then I met a sweet and funny boy just back from the War."

A tender smile appears on her face.

"Brendan Emmett Egan. The love of my life. We got married, had kids, moved here to the suburbs, which meant great happiness for me. But it also meant no time to paint. It's a lot of work raising two boys and taking care of a home. So I stored my talent away in the garage with my old paintings to gather dust."

She sighs. "Maybe, with the boys in college now, I could squeeze in some time to paint. I'll get back to it. Someday."

"Someday? What's wrong with today?" I clap my hand across my mouth. "It's none of my business. I'm sorry, Mrs. Egan."

"No, Remmy, you're right. It's just that I haven't painted in so long, my skills must be rusty. As I've said, being a painter is like being an athlete. You have to use your skills or they weaken. So if I did start again..." Her eyes get wide. "I'm terrified to stand in front of a blank canvas. That big white rectangle staring back at me. What if I've lost my talent entirely?"

I don't say anything. I can tell she's talking to herself, not to me. Mrs. Egan settles back into her pose, but she seems to be somewhere else.

I start painting again. I'm glad I had finished her eyes before our discussion because now they are far away. And her mouth has a sadness.

THE BLANK CANVAS OF FEAR!

Out the window, the sky is filling with a purple-gray blanket of storm clouds. Even though I still have more work to do, I don't want to walk home in the rain. Mrs. Egan agrees to let me finish up the next week and says to run along. I can leave my canvas and supplies in the attic.

I'm sure she would rather be alone now anyway.

25 • The Storm

That blanket of clouds follows me home, growing darker and bigger and forcing me to speed up my footsteps. Rumbles of thunder chase me so that I sprint through my front door just as the first plops of rain hit the sidewalk.

The rain pelts the house. Lightning flashes, followed by big booms of thunder. Mom flies into action like a mother hen flapping her wings. She scurries around, unplugging everything electric, and then corrals Dad and me away from the supposed danger of the large glass picture window and onto the stairway that leads to the second floor. The three of us huddle, perched on the stairs in dark safety, like chickens.

"Angela, this is crazy. If the house is going to get hit by lightning, sitting on the stairs is not going to stop it." A flash lights up Dad's frowning face and he wriggles on the stair.

"We're protecting ourselves," Mom says. "Remember when the Durkin's toilet got hit by lightning? The glass window shattered and the bathroom wallpaper was singed beyond repair."

"Well, I wasn't planning to sit there. I should be downstairs in my chair watching the Yankees game."

"TV is even worse!" Mom pushes Dad's shoulder. "Water and electrical things attract lightning."

Where do mothers get this kind of information? Is there a *Mother's Encyclopedia of Essential Family Knowledge* somewhere or maybe *The Ultimate Mother's Guide to Worry*?

The living room blazes bright for a second and then goes dark, followed by a boom of thunder. The light show repeats over and over, faster and faster. The time between lightning and cracks of thunder gets shorter and soon the storm is raging right over us. I have to admit our huddling feels comforting.

A long flash of lightning and a super-loud thunder boom makes us all jump, even Dad.

"Cripes, that was close!"

"See, Sal? See why we need to sit here?" Mom rubs my back.

"If that bolt had hit us, we'd be fried chicken anyway," Dad grumbles, but he's not leaving the stairs.

"Well, thanks Dad. That's comforting," I say.

More big cracks and rumbles rattle the windows, making us chickens huddle even closer.

Finally, the thunder claps move farther away. But as they get fainter and the rain stops, a new sound is heard—the loud howling of fire engines.

I open the front door and the smell of burning wood fills my nostrils. I suddenly feel an emptiness, a loss, an ache. Something isn't right.

I slam the door shut and race down the streets of my neighborhood following the nasty smell and the sounds of loud yelling and roaring engines and rushing water. I turn a corner and freeze.

Oh, no!

No, no, no, no, no!

Crackling angry flames are devouring Mrs. Egan's yellow garage.

Firemen aim powerful jets of water at the building and billows of smoke rise into the sky.

I run closer, but the scorching heat of the flames pushes me back to the other side of the street where neighbors stand watching the spectacle—their faces lit up by the fire.

Mrs. Egan, wet eyes glued to the fire, stands there with Mr. Egan's arms around her. I slowly approach her and touch her arm. She flinches, sees me, and pulls me into a hug.

"They're all gone, Remmy," she sobs. "A bolt of lightning and they are all gone. All my paintings. All your paintings."

With a crash, the garage roof collapses, sending fiery plumes into the air. The crowd cringes in one loud gasp.

All my paintings. All my dreams. All my hopes. And Mrs. Egan's paintings and memories.

Burning. Melting. Gone in a flash.

The loss of my paintings wallops me in the heart. Months of

work gone. Nothing to show in the Art Awards. Why is this happening?

"Rosella!" Mom and Dad run towards me.

I suddenly know exactly why this is happening. I run to Dad, holding him around the waist, with my face buried in his chest. I sob and sob. He tentatively puts his arms around me.

"I'm so sorry. I'm so sorry I went behind your back." I look up at his confused face. "This is all my fault and this is my punishment and I deserve it and I'll never do it again."

Mom pulls me away from Dad and grabs me by the shoulders. "No, sweetie, this is not a punishment. The storm was just an act of God. An accident."

"Exactly! An act of God! See Mom. God's punishing me for disobeying Dad."

"Would you two tell me what's going on?" Dad says.

Mom takes his arm and holds my hand. "Let's all go home. We have a lot to talk about."

I look back and see Mrs. Egan has turned away from the fire and dissolved into her husband's arms. I also see the flash of a bicycle and flames light up Bill's face.

* * * * *

Mom holds my hand as I cry on the living room couch. I keep my head down otherwise I'd see the Three Heavenly Catholics glaring at me from the dining room. I can't face Dad either but I feel him frowning at me from his chair. I hiccup deep breaths while confessing all that has happened since January: the Art Awards...Mrs. Zabriskie's chores...painting lessons...Mrs. Egan... my paintings hidden in the garage...

I keep sniffing and wiping my nose on my arm.

"Rosella, stop that," Dad says. "Go get yourself a tissue."

When I leave to get one in the bathroom, I hear Mom's high-pitched whisper yelling at Dad.

I walk back into the living room, honking my nose, and the whispering stops.

Mom gives Dad the eye and nods toward me.

"Look, Rosella," he says. "You found a way to take lessons without my help and I have to admit that was pretty resourceful of you."

He glances at Mom and shakes his head. "But you disobeyed my orders. It's tragic your work was ruined, but I still can't support you wanting to be an artist. I've already explained why, and you should have respected my wishes."

Dad pauses.

"I've decided not to punish you since this fire, this act of God, has already caused you enough pain. And since your mother was an accomplice in this scheme..."

Mom fiddles with her pearl necklace.

Dad grunts and heads downstairs to the playroom to watch what's left of the Yankees game.

That's it. My dream is over. My Spark flamed up and destroyed me. I'm burned, melted, turned to ash. I'm just a pile of nothing.

"I'm so sorry, sweetie." Mom pats my hand.

I still have nothing to say. I'm too stunned.

"You know, Nonna always told me she was very proud of Giocomo's talent and gladly supported his dream. Your father refuses to believe that. He was hurt too much. All he saw was how hard his mother worked and how tired she was."

Mom strokes my hair. "He was a little boy and couldn't see the joy in Nonna's heart. But she loved Giocomo and his art more than anything."

Mom puts her arm around my shoulders and I hug her. I remember Nonna's words...*Giocomo would be so proud.*

"And you know what? I didn't actually get your paint box at a rummage sale." Mom smiles and looks me in the eyes. "It belonged to Giocomo. Nonna had kept it and then I saved it for you."

I let this new information sink in. It makes total sense. I knew I felt a connection to that worn old wood box and its years of paint stains. I'm able to smile. Just a little.

Then I remember that the paint box and Mrs. Egan's portrait are still safe inside her attic! They weren't destroyed by the fire.

I still have my Vision of the Year 2000!

That has to mean something.

26 • Goodbye

Two days later, my Super Secret Sketchbook sits open on my lap. I rub the opal charm on my necklace and it feels warm. But deep inside, I ache as if my Spark has been smothered and is barely struggling to stay alive.

Losing my paintings feels like I've lost friends—good friends I created and loved and were unique to me. I miss them, and want back those images and colors and textures. But they've turned to ashes and I have to accept that they're gone and I need to say goodbye.

I pick up my pen and face the blank page. I draw a small field bordered by old trees and place rectangles standing in the grass, some straight, some a little crooked. Each rectangle becomes a painting I lost—my very first painting of a bowl of fruit in shades of gray, a basket of vegetables that started in burnt sienna tones

and then turned colorful by thin glazes of reds and greens and yellows, my first full-color painting of a vase stuffed with sunflowers, the crazy group of mismatched pots of ceramic, copper, glass, and tin that Bill and I painted after finding those naked paintings in the garage, and that final painting of the dogwood blossoms in the crystal vase.

This is my Cemetery of Lost Paintings. This is where I can mourn and visit with my lost friends and remember all that I learned and loved by creating them. The Three Heavenly Catholics in the dining room would approve.

I had committed to winning the Anthony Van Emburgh Art Awards. An act of God destroyed my paintings. I can either take that as a sign to give up or I can rise from the ashes to victory. Both choices feel difficult and painful.

I won't give up. I have to pull myself together and salvage what I can to exhibit at the Art Awards in three weeks. I flip through my Super Secret Sketchbook looking for possible pieces.

Flip, flip, flip. My new year's treasure chest (too personal). Flip, flip, flip. Mrs. Zabriskie's dog Fluffy (no way). Flip, flip. My self-portraits (barf). Flip, flip, flip. Spring flowers (maybe). Flip, flip. My favorite Beatle Paul (yes). Flip. My second favorite Beatle Ringo (maybe).

I keep flipping until I come to the place where a page had been ripped out. Debbie! Her portrait had been here.

I know what I have to do.

Down behind the stairs in the basement, I open the trunk, unlock the suitcase, unzip the sweater bag, unfold sheets of tissue paper, and pull out the fateful portrait of Debbie. Seeing it again after such a long time, I'm impressed by how good it is. The sparkle in her eyes, her bright smile and dimple. I don't see a big fatso. A blimp. A hippo. I see my pretty friend. My pretty *former* friend. This drawing started the beginning of the end.

Debbie hates her portrait, but this piece can make the difference between winning or losing the award. I have to display it. Besides, she won't go to the exhibit so she won't even know.

My Vision of the Year 2000 is still in Mrs. Egan's attic with my paint box. I need to get them, but the thought of seeing the charred collapsed garage and seeing poor Mrs. Egan makes me dizzy and nauseous. The pain she's feeling must be a hundred times worse than mine. All that work and memories.

The next day, I hear Mom and Mrs. Egan talking downstairs. She's brought my painting and paint box, but I stay in my room. I still can't face her and the loss we've both had.

28 • And the Winner Is...

This is it. I thought this would be the night that the Anthony Van Emburgh Art Awards would prove to the world that a girl can be a winner and that girl would be me. But, without my oil paintings, the chance of that happening is zero.

My only hope is that my Vision of the Year 2000 will triumph as the most creative look into the future.

I slowly survey the cafeteria. It's so weird to be in this room at night with the bright florescent lights above and blackness out the windows. Parents, boys in suits and ties, and girls in dresses mill around to check out the Art Awards entries. I had timidly asked Dad to come here after work, but he only made a noncommittal grunt.

One ninth-grade girl has a nice display of her pottery. Mom is chatting with another girl who is showing aprons she sewed and decorated with paint and embroidery. I hope Mom doesn't ask me to make something like that. I mean there's art and then there's Art.

An Oreo crunches in my mouth, and I clutch a paper cup of red punch in my hand. I skulk over to Bill's portfolio display to size up the competition. He's hung his painting of the dogwood flowers in the cut crystal vase, and the one of the group of pitchers that Mrs. Egan had set up on the day Bill and I found those paintings. A hot flush travels up my neck to my face and I can feel my paintings of the same subjects melting in the fire.

I look away and examine two experimental paintings Bill has done in the style of his hero Picasso—a cubist collage of a guitar and a cubist portrait of a girl with long black hair and amber eyes, titled *Mademoiselle*. That can't be The Rat Fink!

Bill's Vision of the Year 2000 is (big surprise!) a self-portrait, with his seventh-grade face aged into his future vision of himself— a man with silver hair proudly gazing at a portrait of himself holding a palette and standing at an easel. A self-self-portrait. Is he mimicking Mr. Van Emburgh's pose in the portrait outside the art room just to earn brownie points? Bill really is his own biggest fan. His ego can fill a whole museum.

"Bill's work sure is good," says a voice. "He may be the winner tonight."

I turn and stare right into Peter's hazeliscious eyes and thoughts of Bill instantly disintegrate. I grin and hope my new red dress makes an impression on Peter. I don't want him to only think of me as having a "good arm."

167

"Ye, hm gud pintig," I mumble, some Oreo crumbs spitting out of my mouth onto Peter's shirt. I take a big swallow of punch to wash down the rest of the cookie. "Oh! Oh, I'm so sorry."

Peter laughs and brushes the crumbs off.

"Forget it. Come see my sculpture. It's my Vision of the Year 2000."

He grabs my free hand and pulls me over to a silver spaceship with flashing lights. He drops my hand and looks lovingly at his sculpture. I look lovingly at him, my hand tingling.

I pull my eyes away from Peter's face and look closely at his spaceship. It's made from many sizes of tin cans, pipes, nuts, bolts, wires, springs, and Christmas lights.

"Wow, that's so cool." It really is. I'm not just saying that because he's Peter. "So you want to be a sculptor?"

"No, but probably an industrial designer. You know, designing things like cars, or maybe even spaceships. See?"

The display panel of his portfolio has drawings of futuristic flying cars, underwater trains, and highways going through and around tall, sleek buildings.

"That's my portfolio over there," I say.

He follows me across the room and I sheepishly stand in front of my panel, thinking about what's missing.

Peter glances around my portfolio, nodding and smiling politely at my spring flowers, and Beatle portraits.

"Hey, that's pretty good." Peter nods at the not-hippo Debbie drawing. "It's your friend, right?"

"Um, yeah. Sort of."

MY VISION OF THE YEAR 2000

I'm not getting into my sad saga of broken friendship.

Then he stops at my Vision of the Year 2000. Mrs. Egan's portrait.

"Who's that in front of Dairy Dream?"

Peter means the white building I painted behind Mrs. Egan.

"Hey, I know that face." Bill appears and butts in. "What's Mrs. Egan doing in front of Dairy Dream?"

I glare from Bill to Peter and back to Bill.

"Why would I paint someone in front of an ice cream store? That white building is the White House in Washington, D.C.! Isn't it obvious?"

Peter thinks for a minute. "Oh. So she's a tour guide at the White House? What does that have to do with the Year 2000?"

I breathe deeply, counting to five. I can't even make it to ten.

"In my Vision of the Year 2000, this is the President of The United States...a WOMAN!"

They both step back, eyes big. A long silence. Then they explode with laughter.

"Are you crazy?" Bill has tears in his eyes. "That could never happen."

Peter's still laughing.

"Of course, it could happen!" The jerks! I don't care how hazeliscious Peter is.

Then I hear a shrieking cackle behind me.

"Debbie! Come here. It's you!"

Oh no, another jerk. The Rat Fink. I push her aside and stand in front of Debbie's portrait to hide it. What are they doing here anyway? Curses! I forgot Jacques has a portfolio hanging.

Debbie is two inches from my face, yelling, "How could you hang this here for the whole school to see? You've humiliated me! I'm so glad I'm not your friend anymore."

Debbie pulls the portrait off the panel, scrunches it into a ball, and throws it on the floor. She storms out of the cafeteria, The Rat Fink right behind her, who turns and gives me a snotty grin.

Bill and Peter quickly disappear into the crowd.

Mom rushes over and hugs me. I try to squeeze out of her arms.

"Mom! Not here." Okay, my mommy hugging me feels real good right now, but I'm in junior high and I break away.

Then I see him.

Dad. He's here!

Dad walks over to my display, bends to pick up the crumpled Debbie, smooths it out, and tacks it back up on the board. He walks away to the refreshment table and I smile at his back, so touched by his gesture I could burst.

Mom guides me out into the hallway.

"Do you want to go home, sweetie?" she asks.

I do.

Instead I say "No, I need to wait for the awards announcement." But no award can outdo the pride I feel right now. Dad's here. He unscrunched Debbie and hung her back up.

Peeking back into the cafeteria from the hallway, I see my display panel. I hope to see expressions of delight and admiration from the general public, not like the reaction of those two laughing

171

hyena boys. But the general public also seems to be giggling and snickering at my Vision.

Mr. Neel makes an ear-piercing whistle and calls everyone to gather around. It's finally time for the big announcement. He introduces a curly-haired woman as Anthony Van Emburgh's great-granddaughter. She waves the envelopes that hold the winners' names and their savings bonds. Principal Schlafly stands by looking grumpy and bored.

"We'll start with third place." Mr. Neel opens the first envelope.

"Leo Parker!" A vaguely-familiar-looking eighth grader whoops while everyone applauds.

Well, I don't want third place anyway.

"And, in second place, we have...Bill Appleton!" Bill is all grins and waves his arms. When he takes his envelope, he kisses it, and waves it at me.

He shouldn't be so smug. Gee, maybe first place is mine after all. Yes, maybe it is. It must be.

It isn't.

It belongs to Bobby Pizzelli, a big-shot ninth grader. Bill looks daggers at Bobby for beating him. And me, I was beat by all of them.

"That leaves the special award for the most creative Vision of the Year 2000," says Mr. Neel. "Principal Schlafly, Miss Van Emburgh, and I had a very difficult time deciding whose Vision best represents the hopes and dreams of America's future."

This is my last chance. *My* hopes and dreams are with the women of America. I cross my fingers and bite my lip. Please, please, please.

"Our Vision for the Year 2000 is..."

I suck in my breath.

"Peter McCleary for his fantastic spaceship!"

It's over.

No woman president.

No fame for me.

No triumph.

Bill's right. Girls are losers. I'm a loser.

My Spark is extinguished.

This time, I do let Mom hug me.

Dad drives us home in silence. The pain I'm feeling from my loss is greater and more discouraging than any lecture Dad can give me at this point.

28 • Don't Bother Me

My heart is as heavy as a meteorite fallen to Earth. I numbly drift through the last two weeks of school as quietly and invisibly as possible, like the Ghost of Seventh Grade Past. Even my opal charm has lost its sparkle. I float through hallways, in and out of classes, avoiding all eyes—especially the ones belonging to Bill, Peter, Debbie, and The Rat Fink.

Debbie avoids me like usual, but I feel The Rat Fink lurking in dark corners like an evil presence. Once in a while, Bill pops up with a "Hey, Miss Rembrandt! How's it going?" I float right through him and keep going. When Peter says "Hi," it's so hard to not look at those dreamy hazeliscious eyes. But I silently move past him, and haunt the hallways in solitude and sorrow.

* * * * *

Finally, school's out for the summer and I retreat to my bedroom for the rest of my miserable life.

I go to the WOW!Wall and take down everything that is art—all the prints and postcards of artists' work. I can't bear to throw any of them out so I pack them all up, plus my portfolio pieces including de-crumpled Debbie, in the sheets of tissue paper and put them away inside the sweater bag, inside the suitcase, inside the trunk under the basement stairs. Maybe never to see the light of day. Ever.

The only things left on the Wow!Wall are Beatles pictures, souvenirs, some magazine pages, photos, and baseball cards. With my humiliation on the baseball field, I decide those cards have to go, too. So long, Mickey. Take care, Yogi. Later, Whitey.

I'm not sure what to do with the watercolor portrait I did of my fave Beatle, Paul McCartney. Is it art or Beatles stuff? I decide on Beatles stuff since the WOW!Wall is now 67% empty. I'll be able to fill the space pretty easily with more Beatles stuff. Maybe one of these days I'll actually leave my self-imposed exile and walk to Woolworth's to get more Beatles magazines and cards.

Or maybe it can wait until next week.

Or the week after that.

Or maybe never.

I play "Don't Bother Me" on my record player. Yeah, just go away, leave me alone. As soon as the Beatles song is over, I pick up the arm and put it at the beginning of the groove and play it again.

And again.

And again.

The blank leatherette-covered sketchbook from Mrs. Egan sits on my dresser, waiting for me. Keep drawing, she had said. We need the exercise. She wants to see what inspires us this summer.

I yank open a drawer and shove the sketchbook under my socks. This is not going to be a summer for inspiration.

* * * * *

Mom calls from downstairs, "Sweetie, phone call!"

I flop on my bed and cover my ears.

"C'mon, you have to leave your room sometime."

Phooey, I can still hear her.

"It's been 5 days. That's long enough. Get down here!"

Mom hands me the phone when I shuffle into the kitchen.

"It's Mrs. Egan," Mom whispers.

What does she want?

"Hello?"

"Remmy, hi. How's your summer going?" she asks me.

"Okay."

"You don't sound very excited. Thought you'd be happy school's out."

I don't answer.

"Have you been using your sketchbook?"

"No. Not really."

"Oh." She hesitates. "I'm so sorry about the Art Awards. I called you a few times, but your mother said you wouldn't come to the phone."

"Yeah, well. It's no big deal." I'm so glad Mrs. Egan couldn't go to the ceremony that night. The humiliation was bad enough in front of all those jerks.

"Look," She uses an annoyingly chipper voice. "I have a big surprise for you, but you can't see it until the Fourth of July Festival in town."

What kind of surprise? I think that in my head, but don't say it out loud.

"Remmy? Will you promise me you'll come to the Festival?"

But that will take time away from my wallowing in self-pity.

"Maybe."

"Please try. I promise it will be worth it!"

29 • Festival Surprise

The Fourth of July Festival seems extra crowded this year which makes me regret being here. It's aggravating trying to weave in and out between families and strollers, shuffling old people, running little boys, and yacking teenage girls followed by teenage boys. If I don't find Mrs. Egan soon, I'm out of here.

I drag my way up the sunny hot street, occasionally getting bopped in the face by some little kid's balloon. I carefully maneuver around Auntie Amy's Krafts booth, the Engine Company No. 8 fire truck, and Signore Pulcinello's Petting Zoo. Mrs. Egan told me to look for her in the art exhibit area.

I pass booths with handmade jewelry, paintings of dogs, wood carvings, until I finally come to a booth with a sign that says "Margaret Egan, Paintings."

The inside of the booth holds a huge surprise. It's chock full of paintings! Bright paintings. Colorful paintings. Bold paintings. Paintings of flowers. Paintings of houses and fields. Paintings of fruit. Paintings of people.

"What do you think?" Mrs. Egan is glowing.

It takes me a while to process what I'm seeing. There's so much to look at that my eyes bounce around the booth. These paintings are nothing like the paintings lost in the fire. They have modern energy and freshness.

"Oh, Mrs. Egan." I look from canvas to canvas to canvas. "These are amazing! You did all these?"

"I sure did." She surveys the booth. "As devastating as the garage fire was, it was the catalyst I needed to move my derrière and start painting again. And you made this happen. You were totally right. There's no point in waiting for Someday. Someday is Today." She gives me a big hug.

Margherita Morandi's medal hangs on display, newly polished. It survived the fire! Margherita Morandi has been reborn into a colorful, vibrant new world and I helped make it happen. It feels great to feel great again.

A bright flash of yellow catches my eye and I'm drawn to a painting titled "Sunflower Symphony." Next to a painting of red geraniums is another patch of red. My "Vision of the Year 2000" is hanging with a red dot on the frame.

"How did my painting get here? And my painting sold?!"

"Your mom snuck it out to me, and yes, it has sold."

That's too impossible to believe, but I'm not so sure I want someone else to own my painting, my Vison of the Year 2000, my

manifesto for the future. It means so much to me. It survived.

But then it hits me and I understand what she's done.

"Oh Mrs. Egan, you didn't have to buy it to make me feel good. I'll give it to you for nothing."

She laughs and shakes her head. "As much as I would love to have the honor of hanging my presidential visage in my home, I didn't buy it."

"Who would buy the laughing stock of the Anthony Van Emburgh Art Awards?" This is the worst kind of a joke.

"I'll show you who." Mrs. Egan calls to an artist in the booth across from hers. "Antoinette, I want you to meet Remmy!"

A familiar-looking woman with curly hair comes over and shakes my hand.

"Remmy, I just loved your painting the minute I saw it at the Art Awards—not just for your accomplished technique, but for the absolutely brilliant concept, too," she says.

I'm startled by the praise from this stranger. Is she a junior high parent? Why else would she have been at the Awards?

She must see the confusion in my face. "I'm Anthony Van Emburgh's great-granddaughter. I was one of the judges."

Swell, one of the judges who rejected me. She's just teasing me. This humiliation never ends.

"I was fighting to give the Vision award to you, but those two big lugs outvoted me," Miss Van Emburgh says. "They were totally dazzled by that shiny symbol of the space age."

I laugh thinking of Mr. Neel and Mr. Schlafly as big lugs. "Thanks for buying my painting."

"Your painting is the perfect symbol for the future of America, and all the women who yearn for equality. I'm going to hang it in my office. I'm president of the Village Arts Council."

Wow. Finally. Someone understands my vision.

"I'm so glad we got to meet, but I have to get back to my booth and sell some of my own paintings." Miss Van Emburgh winks. "Keep painting. Never give up!"

"No. I never will. Thanks!"

I watch her curly hair bounce as she walks away.

Some people try to push past me to look at Mrs. Egan's work, so I decide to check out the rest of the Festival.

I ramble up the street, passing people gawking at antique cars, eating hot dogs, and throwing darts at balloons to win prizes.

A cardboard Eiffel Tower perches precariously on top of a booth decorated with French flags. A clump of junior high kids underneath the canopy jabber away in French. I spot Debbie standing alone cutting up slices of strange yellow pie. I'm tempted to go to buy a piece when I hear that loud cackle. The Rat Fink runs up to Debbie and gives her a kiss on each cheek and they crack up.

No. No pie for me.

I dash back towards the antique cars, hide behind a Model-T, and sit down on its running board. I gulp for air and my vision is blurred by tears. I shouldn't still hurt. The friendship is over.

I sense a presence looming over me, blocking the hot sun.

"Hi, Miss Rembrandt. Long time no see." Bill sits down next to me on the running board.

I turn away from him and quickly wipe my tears. "Oh, I've been pretty busy this summer."

"I was just at Mrs. Egan's booth. She said you were around here somewhere."

He came looking for me?

"Her new paintings are so awesome! Even with no naked people," Bill laughs.

I can't hold in a laugh and face him. "Yeah, they're pretty incredible."

"And I saw that your Vision 2000 painting sold. That's so cool. Your first sale." Bill pushes his long bangs out of his face. "You know, I laughed at the crazy idea. A lady president?!"

He may not see the future, but Miss Van Emburgh does.

"But besides the concept, I thought your painting was really well done. Especially the skin tones and her expression."

"Thanks." He's being kind of nice, for such a goofball.

"Oh! And can you believe it? The contest!" Bill jumps to his feet. "I just heard the news this morning and thought you must be going as ape as I am!"

"News? What news? What contest?" Not much can make me go ape.

"You're kidding, right?" he asks.

"No. What? What?"

"WABC Radio announced they're having a Draw-the-Beatles contest. I can't believe you didn't hear. All the winners get tickets to the Beatles concert in August."

I jump to my feet. "Holy John-Paul-George-and-Ringo! I am

going ape!" Instantly, art ideas start popping into my mind. "I have to see the Beatles! I have to win!"

"Can you imagine winning?" Bill says. "That would be insane."

My stomach turns as I relive that disastrous night in the cafeteria. How can I compete again with Bill? Plus all of New York and New Jersey and maybe even Connecticut? All that torture and anxiety. But now the stakes are even higher. The Beatles! I have to win. I have to! I just have to!

My knees start to buckle and Bill grabs my arm to hold me up.

"Are you okay?" He actually looks concerned.

We lock eyes and smile. This feels nice.

"Looks like we're competing again." My arm tingles where Bill held me.

"Looks like." He steps back from me, but is still smiling.

"Oh," Bill breaks the trance. "My guitar class will be playing some tunes up at the band shell at 1:00."

He waves a guitar case at me. He must have finally given up on sports and found a better way to act cool.

"Stop by." He grins and starts to walk away. "Good luck with the contest, Miss Rembrandt. May the best Beatlemaniac win!"

"I will!" I shout as he leaves to join the crowd. "I'll stop by AND I'll win!"

I watch until he disappears.

Then I think of that other Beatlemaniac. Debbie.

When we first saw the Beatles on *The Ed Sullivan Show* on February 9, 1964, The Night That Changed Music Forever, we made that cross-your-heart-and-hope-to-die pledge that someday we would see the Beatles together. She has to remember that. Debbie would go bananas at this concert. I just have to win.

30 • A Dreamy Idea

With only three days left to get my Beatles contest entry to the post office, the pressure is on. I've been doodling around in my Super Secret Sketchbook for a week and haven't found THE IDEA.

After an energy-filled dinner of chicken parmesan, I lock myself in my room and won't come out until I've got a winner. Holding my opal necklace charm, I summon my Spark of an Artist so inspiration will snap and pop and fuel this crucial creation.

I scatter Beatles magazines and cards all over my bed, looking for an award-winning idea. I group cards into themes—all four lads in one photo, individual photos of each lad, goofing-around photos, color photos.

What medium should I use? Maybe if I use an unusual medium and unique style, my entry will stand out. I pull out a piece of black construction paper and white chalk. Looking at a picture of Paul from a magazine, I use the chalk to draw in only the highlights, so that the black paper becomes the shadows of the portrait.

Chalk-dust clouds fill the air.

"Aaaaahhhhchooo! Aahchoo!"

I sneeze and cough and drop the chalk on the paper. I try to grab it, and my hands leave smears of white fingerprints all over the portrait. What a mess! I rip the black paper into shreds.

New plan.

If I want to really impress the judges, I need to draw all four Beatles, not just my fave. I get out a large sheet of paper (white this time), and pick the dreamiest card for each Beatle. I can combine them all together somehow in one drawing.

I stare at the blank paper, then at the cards, then at the paper, then at the cards. My brain is full of dead ends. Now I understand why Mrs. Egan was so afraid to face an empty canvas.

WOW!Wall, help me!

My shrine to the Beatles is growing on the WOW!Wall and I pray for inspiration. What else inspires me? Alfred E. Neuman grins from a cover of *Mad* magazine and reminds me of his motto: "What, me worry?" I'm trying not to worry, but I'm starting to panic.

My eyes zero in on some *Peanuts* comic strips. I love *Peanuts*, maybe because of Snoopy. I've always wanted a dog, especially if he had thought balloons coming out of his head. Maybe these comics will be the answer.

Holy Beatles Tickets! A *cartoon* won't impress the judges.

Gaaaaa! I stretch my arms out and take a flying leap onto my bed. Cards and magazines scatter and I duck my head under the pillow. What can I make? What can I draw? I squeeze my head with the pillow. Think! Think! Inspiration find me!

I turn over and throw the pillow off my bed. I take a deep breath and let all my muscles go limp. Why did I think I could win this contest? I can't do this. I can't win. I can't see the Beatles in concert. I close my eyes for what seems like a couple of minutes.

I'm standing on a hill watching a night sky filled with waves and swirls of every possible color of blue. The sky whirls over New York City and holds rings of yellow stars and the Moon. The Empire State Building rises out of the landscape like a rocket. Like the dream I had months ago, I'm experiencing Vincent van Gogh's painting, The Starry Night, *but with a totally different scenario.*

As I watch the dramatic sky, fragments of music stream from the colorful swirls. Then clouds drift in and faces emerge—Paul's dreamy eyes, John's ironic grin, Ringo's distinctive nose, George's dancing eyebrows.

The sky has become a heavenly concert full of delight and excitement, and pulsates with melodies and harmonies.

I bolt awake. This is it! Before my dream dissolves from my mind, I squeeze my eyes shut and commit it to memory so I can recreate it all on canvas. I've got THE IDEA!

I pull my grandfather's paint box out of my closet and set up a canvas and my palette of paint. My Spark is blazing with inspiration (and maybe some divine help from Giocomo) as I recreate my Beatles dream that may make my *actual* dream of seeing them in concert come true.

* * * * *

The next morning, before packing up my painting, I walk it past the Three Heavenly Catholics in the dining room and they smile with approval. Then I stand at the edge of the living room and try to read the mood of the room.

Sinatra is singing on the hi-fi about strangers and night while Mom hums along, knitting something fuchsia and fuzzy. Dad's nose is in the newspaper like usual. It all seems fairly non-confrontational, so I sidle over to Mom to give her a peek at my entry.

"Oh sweetie. This is beautiful." She pushes her wool creation into her knitting bag and takes the painting. "All the colors and movement. And Beatles, too."

Mom stands and walks over to Dad.

Is she kidding? Dad will toss my painting across the room like a Frisbee. I step forward in case I need to jump for my flying art and race it to the post office.

"Sal, you must see this. It's for a contest." Mom says, pulling away Dad's newspaper, which is an act daring enough to make him explode.

But instead, he takes my painting and examines it for quite

awhile. I chew my thumbnail waiting for a reaction.

Dad looks at me. "This reminds me of that big starry painting in the museum."

"Yes," I say. "By Vincent van Gogh."

He hands the painting to me and retrieves his newspaper to start reading again.

Where is the lecture? The disapproval? The Henry VIII grumbling?

His silence is as good as a big booming cheer and my heart leaps. Mom gives me a wink and I race to my room to pack up my entry. I just won a glimmer of acceptance from Dad. I hope the Beatle contest judges are even more accepting.

31 • Waiting For News

My transistor radio sings "Seventy-seven...W-A-BEATLE-CEEEEEEE," but then dissolves into static. I wiggle the antenna and rotate the radio, trying to pull in the signal. Holy moly! When are they going to make the announcement about the contest? It's been eleven long days since I mailed in my entry and today's the day the radio station is notifying the winners.

Sitting under the baby maple tree in my front yard, I tuck my legs under me to squeeze into the tiny patch of shade. I wipe sweat off my forehead and smack the radio trying to get the signal.

"Lonely. I'm Mr. Lonely..." the radio sings. Ugh. I'd turn off this sappy song but I'm afraid to miss the announcement.

My stomach flip-flops the same way it did when I waited for the Vision of the Year 2000 to be announced at the Art Awards. Why did I put myself through this again? Of course to see the

Beatles, but also to beat Bill? To prove myself to Dad? Yes. And no. Honestly, if I were stranded on a desert island with art supplies with no one around to impress, I'd still have to make art.

When the whiney singing stops, I stand up to stretch my legs, readjusting the volume on the radio so I can hear the DJ better.

"Big Dan Ingram here, laughin' and scratchin'," he cheers.

Come on Big Dan, announce the winners! Oh, now he's talking about the weather. Yeah, it's hot, Big Dan. Get to the important stuff.

Next door, Debbie's house sits quiet until the front door flies open. I can't hide behind our tree. It's too skinny. But I'm safe. It's just Debbie's bratty brother and his bratty friend who fly down the front steps and head to the woods.

I slump back down under the tree and put my ear to the radio. "I'm Henerey the Eighth I am..." Herman's Hermits sing. That Herman is so cute and closer to my age than my true love Paul, but I'm forever devoted to my fave Beatle. I close my eyes and see Paul's puppy dog eyes until they turn into Peter's hazeliscious eyes which I haven't seen since school closed for the summer.

"Remmy!"

Mom's waving from the front door and the spell of the eyes breaks.

"Sweety! Hurry! A phone call for you."

This has to be the news I'm waiting for. They must be calling winners instead of announcing it on the radio. I scramble to the house, clutching my transistor radio.

"Hello?" I croak into the phone.

"Hi, Miss Rembrandt."

Curses! It's just Bill.

"Oh, it's just you."

"Nice to talk to you, too."

I don't have time to be polite. "We have to get off the phone. I'm waiting for a very important call."

"Yeah, well so am I." Bill says. "I'm going crazy. Call me if you hear anything, okay?"

I hang up. Bill's going to win. I know it.

Should I go back outside? I might as well because, if I stay and stare at the phone, it won't ring. And if it does ring, it will be Bill gloating.

The phone rings and I grab it.

"Bill, did you hear something? Did you win?"

"Hello? Is this Remmy?" It's a woman's voice, not Bill's.

"Yes, it is."

"This is Mrs. Bernstein from WABC Radio." My breath stops. "You are one of the winners in our Draw-the-Beatles contest! Congratulations."

I nod my head.

"Hello?" Oh. She can't hear my head rattle.

"I won? I won?" The Beatles! I'm going to see the Beatles!

I bounce all over the kitchen, get tangled in the cord, and almost pull the phone off the wall.

"We're having a special awards ceremony on Saturday at the New York World's Fair. Big Dan Ingram will give all you winners your concert tickets. Can you be there?"

"Yes, yes, yes!!!" I'll finally see the World's Fair! If Dad's willing to drive us, that is. Mom will make him. She has to!

Then I have another thought.

"Mrs. Bernstein, do you know if any of the other winners are named Bill?" I hold my breath.

"Umm, let me double check my list. Bill, Bill...No, I don't see any Bills."

"Thank you!!!" I can't decide which is more thrilling—seeing the Beatles or beating Bill and breaking the bad news to him.

When I hang up, I hug Mom, almost knocking her over.

"I WON! I WON! I WON! My art was one of the best and we have to go to the World's Fair to get the tickets and I'm gonna see the Beatles and I bet I meet them."

"I'm so proud of you, sweetie. Wait until Dad gets home. I know he'll be proud."

I think he'll be more flabbergasted than proud. But that doesn't dampen my excitement.

I'm still catching my breath when I automatically grab the phone and start to dial Debbie's number to tell her the incredible news. She won't believe it!

But no. I can't call Debbie.

She isn't the friend who pledged we would see the Beatles together. She isn't the friend I'm taking to the concert. She isn't my friend. Period.

I hang the phone receiver back up.

I don't have the heart to call Bill. Not yet. I thought it would feel so good to beat him, but it doesn't. He's been too nice.

Upstairs in my room, I stand in front of the WOW!Wall. All my Beatles photos are smiling at me, so I smile right back. My dream has come true!

"I'm gonna see you and you and you and you!" The Fab Four are just a excited as I am.

32 • Finally the Fair

The Unisphere comes into view as we speed along the highway through Queens. The steel world globe is 12-stories high, and is the dazzling symbol of the New York World's Fair. I can't take my eyes off it. Finally I'll be seeing The Whole World and The Future. AND getting my Beatles tickets!

We veer off the highway and pull into a parking lot.

"Dad, aren't we awfully far away from the Fair?" I ask. The Unisphere has shrunk in the distance.

"This parking lot costs less than the ones right near the Fair entrance." Dad locks the car. "I'm just trying to make up for the cost of the bridge tolls."

"We're lucky the radio station gave us entry tickets, or we might not even be here at all." Mom gives me a wink. Mom made sure Dad would take us.

199

Hiking towards the Fair, my heart beats faster and faster—not just for the quick walking, but for the excitement of this day.

After we join the crowds of people and pass through the entry of the Fair, Dad pulls out a map.

"Now, we need to find the Better Living Center which is in the Industrial area." Dad buries his nose in the map while I check out the cool buildings that fan out in all directions.

"Look, there's a whole village." People stroll around cobblestone streets, past pointy-topped stone homes and shops. It's like a fairy tale—although seeing the Beatles is the best fairy tale.

"Oh, that must be the Belgian Village. Mrs. Farfalla told me they have these thick waffles with sliced strawberries and whipped cream." Mom licks her lips. "Let's stop there on the way home."

"We need to figure out where to go before we think about food." Dad turns the map over and back again. "Let's walk to the Unisphere and get our bearings."

I check my watch. "Aren't we supposed to be at the awards ceremony by 1:00? It's already 12:30 and this place is huge!"

The view changes quickly as we scramble past other European buildings and into the Space Age. The pavilions in this section have soaring spires, gleaming wings of glass, concrete boxes and towers.

"Rosella, stop right there. I want to take your picture with the Unisphere in the background"

I pose with a forced smile, but my legs are squirming to keep

going. "Come on, Dad. We're going to be late!" I pull him along. "Maybe we should ask somebody where to go."

Mom grabs the map and gives it a quick scan.

"Okay. We need to go through the International area. Let's head this way."

We leave the futuristic United States and enter foreign lands, running past exotic pavilions with minarets, golden temples, pagodas. The air smells of spices, sauces, and sweets.

"Hurry!" Mom runs toward a pavilion with an outdoor deck that bulges and curves like the surface of the moon. One more corner and we enter the Industrial area. I stop in front of a glowing sky-high tower of glass bars until I hear Dad say, "There it is! The Better Living Center."

As we enter the auditorium, I spot a man who must be Big Dan Ingram, the WABC disk jockey, in the flesh! He's on the stage, a microphone in his hand, chatting with a group of kids. My mind had conjured up what he would look like based on his radio voice, but this isn't it. With his trim hair and suit and tie, he looks more like a bank manager than a deejay.

A woman with a clipboard runs up to us. "Remmy?"

I nod, still a bit breathless.

"Hi, I'm Mrs. Bernstein. We were getting worried about you. Why don't you hop up onto the stage while your parents get settled in the audience?" I follow her and she hands me my winning painting. "You won in the 'Most Creative' category."

I look around at the other winners and their artwork. Two boys drew each Beatle life size, standing on each other's shoulders.

Measuring 25 feet high, their art won for the "Largest." A girl had a portrait of Paul's face almost as tall as she is, and won for "Most Realistic." I can't believe how good it was. The girl's long, wavy, dark hair and flowy black dress fit the image of a real artist. I look down at my pink seersucker dress. Maybe I need to start wearing black.

"Hello, Kemosabe!" Big Dan yells into the microphone. Cheers bounce back to him from the audience. "Our WABC Draw-the-Beatles contest brought in thousands of entries. But these eight kids are the big winners! It's time to award two Beatles tickets to each of these fabulous artists."

One by one, the winners are called forward to get their tickets. My stomach churns as I wait for my turn. My sweaty hands tremble. When my name is called, Big Dan hands me an envelope with the tickets and shakes my clammy hand. Camera light bulbs flash and the audience cheers.

"A little nervous, heh?" He wipes his hand on his slacks. "Well, congratulations Remmy and enjoy the concert."

I break into a wobbly smile, overwhelmed by the crowd, the lights, and the reality of seeing the Beatles. Then I inhale, stand tall, and accept my success.

"You've got two tickets there," says Big Dan. "Who's the lucky friend you're taking with you?"

My lucky friend? I feel like Big Dan just punched me in the stomach. It should be Debbie, but it can't be. I'm friendless and I frown. I look down at the precious tickets in my hand.

"Remmy?"

"I don't know." I choke out an answer.

"Oh." Big Dan turns to the audience. "Well, let's hear it for Remmy!" Big Dan raises his arms, the audience politely applauds, and I leave the stage.

Mom gives me one of her comfort hugs.

"This is all very exciting." Dad pats me on the back. "Maybe this art thing is worthwhile after all, Remmy."

Remmy? Dad makes me smile. A big, proud smile.

"So let's go really see this Fair," he says, "now that we don't have to run through it!"

33 • The Beatle Blooper

Only four more days and I'll be seeing the Beatles! The real flesh-and-blood, cuter-than-cute, living and breathing and singing Beatles! And I bet us winners will sit in a special section right up front and after the concert we'll to go backstage and meet them!

The wait is killing me. I can't stop looking at the clock and calendar.

But it's also killing me that I still haven't invited anyone to go with me. The most important event of my entire life and who can I share it with?

I stand at the WOW!Wall looking at a picture of John, Paul, George, and Ringo and imagine meeting my idols. What if I act all silly and then faint and miss the whole encounter? No, I'll be strong and clear-headed and mature. John and Ringo are already married, but Paul and George will be so impressed with me, they'll forget all about their girlfriends Jane and Patti.

I catch a glimpse of myself in the mirror. My perm is now three-quarters grown out so that most of my hair is straight as spaghetti, but the ends are still curling like Slinkys almost reaching my shoulders.

"Gaaaa, this hair!"

Pulling at my hair, I flop onto my bed, bouncing magazines and Beatles cards all around the bedspread.

"Hmmm." I drag a *16 Magazine* closer to me to look at an article that got knocked open. "Get Your Own Beatle Bob," it says, with photos of a hair dresser cutting a girl's hair just like the Beatles. "Neato. That's what I need!"

I grab scissors off my desk and stand in front of the mirror, a big clump of hair in my fist.

"Goodbye, Frizzy. Hello, FAB!" With snip, snip, snips, brown chunks float down and clutter the floor like dead leaves.

"SWEETIE!" Mom stands in the doorway, her mouth open in horror. "What have you done?"

"I cut my own Beatle Bob. What do you think?"

When I spin back to the mirror and get a good look at my creation, a horrible wail escapes my mouth. This is worse than the time I cut my Barbie's blond hair and dyed it orange with food coloring. Uneven spurts of hair crown my head, with longer hanks sticking out the back.

"I can't go to the concert like THIS!" I cry and snort. My nose turns red and pink blotches appear around my eyes.

"I'll call Miss Elayne at Arthur's House of Beauty and see if she can squeeze us in," says Mom. "Go wash your face and we'll get this fixed."

* * * * *

As Mom and I walk up Village Avenue, my disguise hides me from all unwelcome attention. Borrowing from Bill's incognito baseball look, I pulled Dad's Yankee cap down over my ears to hide my butchered coiffeur, wear sunglasses, and skulk along, ten paces behind Mom.

"Hey, Remmy!"

Holy Hairdo. Who spotted me?

Unfortunately, Peter sees right through my spy look. I can barely see his hazeliscious eyes through my dark shades. They must have super powers since they recognized me.

"I heard about the contest. That is so cool you won! You deserve it," he says.

"Thanks," I grunt and dash towards Arthur's House of Beauty.

* * * * *

An hour later, Mom and I emerge from the beauty parlor, my disaster repaired.

"Ooh, the wind is tickling my ears." I tug at the short wisps of hair all over my head. Miss Elayne called this a Pixie hairdo, but it's a Beatle Bob to me.

"It will take some getting used to, but it honestly looks very cute." Mom ruffles the top of my head.

I'm feeling a little less stupid for what I did to my hair thanks to Miss Elayne. At least I didn't also dye it orange like my Barbie.

"May I walk up to Woolworth's and come home later. I need some more pens."

"Okay," Mom hands me a quarter. "Would you also get me a hairnet, brown if they have it. Dad hates the pink ones."

"Sure, see you later." I head up the street, startling myself every time I catch a glimpse of my new hairdo in a store window. Yeah, it'll take getting used to, but I'm feeling kind of hip.

At Woolworth's, I find the hairnet near the hair rollers and then look in the stationary supplies for pens.

"Oh, my gosh! Is that a real Beatle?"

I hear a squeal and a cackle. I turn and face The Rat Fink and her evil amber eyes. It's too late to duck away so I straighten my back and raise my chin.

"I'm an award-winning artist, in case you haven't heard." Let's hear her beat that.

"Yeah, Remmy, congratulations for winning the contest." Debbie appears next to her current friend, a big smile on her face that makes her dimple pop. "You are so lucky to be seeing the Beatles!"

"If she wants to see the Beatles," The Rat Fink interrupts, "all she has to do is look in the mirror. Look at that dopey haircut. It's bad enough you want to play with the boys. Now you look like one."

209

"That's not funny," Debbie says. "Her hair looks nice. Really cute, like from a magazine."

The Rat Fink adds, "Yeah, like maybe from *Mad* magazine."

I glare at them both wishing they would just slink away into the cosmetic aisle.

Debbie smoothes her flip with her hand. "No, Rem, really. Your hair's so stylish. I could do your makeup so you'd look real Mod."

"Oh, you're just trying to butter her up," The Rat Fink pokes my ex-friend in the arm, "so she'll invite you to the concert."

Debbie looks sheepish. She shoves The Rat Fink's shoulder and says, "That's not true! Rem is my oldest friend."

"Well, maybe oldest, but not best." The Rat Fink looks from me to Debbie. "Well, I've got more important things to do. Call me later." The slithery vermin scurries away.

The store is very quiet except for the sound of crickets in the pet department. I look down at my Keds.

"Rem, can I buy you a milk shake at the lunch counter? You know, to celebrate your win? I know you love chocolate."

I look into my ex-friend's eyes. They do seem overly friendly, not like the genuine friendly looks we used to share.

"Remember when the Beatles were first on *Ed Sullivan* and we just screamed and cried?" Debbie asks. "Your Dad thought we were nuts."

"And remember how we went to see *A Hard Day's Night* at the Warner and we sat through it four times until we knew every line by heart?"

Of course, I remember. My favorite group ever and my best friend ever all together. It was thrilling, like history was being made.

"And now you're going to really see them in person." She smiles with expectation.

"Yes, I am." And our friendship is in the past and the pledge we made is broken to bits. That's our reality. I have nothing else to say.

A familiar tall figure with a guitar case lopes by outside the window and I use this as a chance to escape.

"I've got to run," I say and dash out the door and down the sidewalk.

I never called Bill to gloat about the contest. I knew he would be disappointed and I didn't want to rub it in. And then I just chickened out all together.

I yell ahead of me. "Hey!"

Bill turns and frowns when he sees me. He brushes back his long bangs. Is he starting to look like John Lennon?

But then he flashes a wise-guy kind of smile.

"Well, Miss Rembrandt. How does it feel to be a big winner?"

"You ought to know." I wise-guy smile back at him.

"But I think Beatles tickets outrank a lousy savings bond, don't you?"

"They really do." I outrank him!

"Congratulations, Remmy." He called me Remmy. "I guess you're a pretty good artist...for a girl."

He laughs a nice laugh, not a mean laugh. "Really." He touches my arm. "I'm happy for you."

A tingle zips through my stomach. "Uh, thanks."

He can be a pretty nice person...for a boy.

We walk together silently until we reach the Village Music School and Bill goes in for his lesson.

* * * * *

That night, in bed, the big decision races around my brain.

Who should I take to the concert?

Debbie's my oldest friend, my Beatles friend. But she's not a friend anymore although she was pretending to be. And, even though I beat out Bill, he's been pretty nice about it. And he's definitely looking like John Lennon. But I always melt when I see Peter's hazeliscious eyes. Mrs. Egan loves the Beatles, but it'd be kind of weird going with an adult. Although, I might end up taking Mom. Or Dad.

Debbie? Bill? Peter? Mrs. Egan? Mom? Dad? Debbie? Bill? Peter? Mrs. Egan? Mom? Dad? Debbie? Bill? Peter? Mrs. Egan? Mom? Dad? Debbie.....Bill.....Peter.....Mrs. Egan.....Mom.....Dad... ..Deb.....

34 • The Concert

Tonight is the night. THE BEATLES! My heart's pounding like a drum solo as we walk towards Shea Stadium. The building is huge and shiny new and buzzing with excitement.

"Look at the size of this place. I hear there are 55,000 seats." Dad shakes his head. "Its crazy to have a concert in a baseball stadium."

"But I bet every seat is filled," I say.

We join the swelling ocean of fans heading to the entry gates.

"Okay, sweetie, you've got the tickets, right?" Mom asks the same way she asked me before we left the house and then after we got into the car and again as we drove away from the neighborhood.

"Yep, I'm protecting them like I'm an armored truck." I pat my pocket holding the treasure I had won to make sure I really did still have them.

Dad motions to a bench near a chain link fence. "Mom and I are going to wait for you on that park bench over there. Have fun, you two!"

Even at 7:30 at night, the temperature is sweltering and we merge with the sticky crowd of other Beatlemaniacs being herded into the stadium.

Once inside, I catch my breath and smile at Bill. I see that same old twinkle in his eyes like when we made art projects together at Glen Elementary. But now he's twinkling a zillion times brighter. I made the right decision.

"I've never seen so many girls in one place at one time!" Bill says, gawking around at the bouncing, giggling crowd. "It's fun being out-numbered."

I smack his arm. "Well, just pay attention to this girl. You wouldn't be here without me."

"And I'm truly honored to be sharing this experience with you, Miss Rembrandt." He makes a low bow. "Okay, let's figure out where we're sitting,"

"Since I'm a contest winner, we have to be right up front. You know, so close to the stage we can actually see them spit. I hope Paul sees me. I've got my camera, so I can get a great photo of him waving at me." I straighten my Starmite on the cord around my neck. "And I bet we get to meet them backstage and take pictures with them!"

I feel the tiny photo flashbulbs in my pocket. All set.

Suddenly, a surge in the big crowd jostles me. I lose sight of Bill. I spin around, frantic. "BILL!" Where is he? "BILL??!!"

A strong hand grabs my arm and I'm facing my friend again. I'm shaking but now I'm safe.

"You can't sneak away from me that easily. You've got the tickets." Bill firmly takes my hand and I feel that buzzy tingle inside.

"Phooey, you caught me." I laugh and squeeze his hand. "We'd better get in our seats before we miss the show."

We look down a long aisle of seats and see the Mets baseball field blazing in the floodlights.

"Oh, it's so much bigger in person!" I've never been to a major league ball game. It's a shock to see such bright green grass in person instead of the gray grass on TV.

"Wow, the stage is way out on second base," Bill groans. "There's no seating on the field. Just barricades and a ton of police. Nobody will be close enough to see them spit."

"Well, then our seats have to be down there at the edge of the field," I say. "Let's go."

But a burly towering usher stops us.

"Hold up there, princess. Let me see your tickets." He hands back our ticket stubs, and points to an escalator. "Take it upstairs."

I just stare at him. "No, there's a mistake. We're sitting up front, close to the stage."

"Yeah, you and the Queen of England. Just read your ticket, sweetheart. Keep moving." He waves us away.

"But I'm a winner," I whisper.

Bill and I take the escalator to the second deck. The next usher checks our ticket stubs and points to yet another escalator.

"You're kidding!" Bill looks up. "I'm going to get a nose bleed if we go much higher."

Again, we get on another escalator. Finally, the last usher directs us to our seats.

"I should have brought a telescope. It's easier seeing the craters on the moon than that tiny stage." Bill looks up at the sky.

"Why did I even bring a camera?" I slouch in my seat. "We're supposed to have the best seats. It feels like we're up in a helicopter."

As I say that, I hear a pockety-pockety sound and spot a helicopter head over the stadium and toward a roof-top landing on a building in the distance. I elbow Bill and say "I bet that's them. It's got to be them! It won't be long now."

Suddenly, it doesn't matter where our seats are.

At eight o'clock, the whole stadium stands and sings the National Anthem. When an announcer shouts through the loud speaker, "Don't worry. The Beatles are here," the stadium explodes with screams. I've never heard such an ear-piercing sound—some of it coming out of me and Bill.

But the screams lessen when we realize the Beatles aren't coming out right away. First, some discotéque dancers dance to recorded instrumental songs. Then a Motown singer takes her turn performing, followed by five guys in a band. The screaming continues in changing waves of volume depending who's on stage.

"Who are these performers? Have you ever heard of them?" I shout into Bill's ear.

"Heard of them? I can't even just hear them," he shouts back.

Another group performs and then another starts to sing.

"Na na na na na na ..." The audience starts singing along.

"Hey listen. I know this song." I start dancing and Bill joins me.

"Ya know how to pony...mashed potatoes...do the twist... watusi..." We sing with the crowd and do all the dances.

We collapse into our seats, dripping in sweat.

"I thought we were here to see the Beatles," Bill mutters.

I'm thinking the same thing as still another group takes the stage.

FINALLY, after over an hour, IT REALLY IS TIME.

Ed Sullivan comes on to the stage and we scream, knowing why he is here. He yells something about "The Queen" and "America" and then "Here are THE BEATLES!!!!"

I didn't think it could be possible, but the screams get even louder as the Beatles—the ACTUAL Beatles—run out to the second base stage and everyone jumps to their feet.

"I can barely see them. They look like ants instead of Beatles!" Bill shouts.

"Not to me." Even at this distance I can still tell Ringo from George from Paul from John. My eyes are fixed on the stage, and filled with tears.

Ringo beats his drums, Paul plays his left-handed guitar and shares a microphone with George, and John jumps back and forth between guitar and keyboard. They sing and rock and strum and dance so it looks like they're making music. Bill and I bounce and clap to what we think is the music. But it's impossible to hear anything over the nonstop screams.

I strain to hear any familiar notes or words. "I think they're playing 'Ticket to Ride,'" I yell at Bill.

"No, that beat doesn't match the way their guitars are moving," he yells back. "They're playing faster. It looks like 'A Hard Day's Night' to me." He mimics playing a guitar, strumming and moving his fingers up an invisible guitar neck. He has to be right. He's the guitar student.

But hey, it doesn't matter.

The Beatles are here and Bill and I are here. We are all sharing the same steamy night, and breathing the same hot air, and seeing the same stars, and hearing all the music and screaming collide. I'll never forget this. Ever.

When the Beatles take a bow that means a song has ended, so I keep track of how many songs the sing. They break into song number twelve. The crowd must be losing a bit of steam because I can actually kind of hear that they are playing "I'm Down." The Beatles jump around and John goes crazy playing the keyboard with his elbows. Screams explode even louder.

When the Beatles finish this song and take their bows, they run off the stage waving. The screams rise to a deafening pitch. It's only been 30 minutes. The four disappear into a long white car that drives off the field. The whole stadium keeps screaming "NO! NO!"—not wanting it to be over. But it is.

The screams eventually fade and change to happy chatter and

218

some sobbing. The crowd shuffles out and funnels its way down the escalators. I'm hoarse and exhausted and ecstatic as we follow.

We are close to exiting the stadium when Bill pulls me aside. "Remmy."

I look into Bill's eyes. They are unusually large.

"This was totally the best night," he says, then bites his lip.

"Yeah, I know. The best. Can you believe it? We actually saw the Beatles."

"I mean, it was the best because I was with you."

"Oh."

Bill leans closer to me.

I take a step back. "Um, well, I knew you were almost as big a Beatles fan as I am and, you know, who would be better to take and then like Debbie turned out to be such a creep and—"

Bill lurches forward and plants his lips on mine, but then steps on my foot and I let out a yelp. He grabs my arms so I don't fall.

"I'm so sorry!" Bill says. He looks panicky.

"I'm not," I smile, enjoying that buzzy tingle inside.

35 • Just The Beginning

The next week, a knock on my bedroom door startles me and I instinctively slam shut my Super Summer Sketchbook and hold it to my chest.

"Remmy?"

It's Dad.

What am I doing? I loosen my grip on the sketchbook and put it down on my bed. I don't need to hide it from Dad anymore.

"Come in."

Both my parents enter wearing big smiles. Dad's waving something and Mom has a hand behind her back. This puzzling display of happiness is usually reserved for birthdays.

"We've got a surprise for you." Dad hands me a page from the local paper.

I read the headline. "Village Girl Wins Beatles Art Contest."

The article has a picture of me holding my artwork and shaking hands with Big Dan Ingram. "Wow! How did this get into the paper?"

"I got the photo from the radio station and sent it to the newspaper." Dad gives me a big wink. "I wanted to spread the news about my talented artistic daughter."

I tack the article to the WOW!WALL. I'm super proud—a celebrity in my own town. And I'm super proud that Dad is proud.

"Here's one more surprise." Mom hands me a jewelry box with a pictures of the Beatles on the lid and side. It looks like a treasure box. "Go ahead. Open it."

When I lift the lid, a sweet tinkling song plays.

"'She Loves You!' This is so fab. I love it." A Beatles song played by tiny fairy bells instead of guitars still sounds great.

The inside of the box is covered in red velvet.

"You can keep all your treasures in the box," Mom says.

How do moms always know what you're thinking? I started the year anticipating treasures.

But something is already in the box and I lift it out. It is a small, scratched-up paint brush. It seems very old. Many of the sable hairs are missing, but the remaining feel soft.

"That belonged to your grandfather," Dad says. "I saved it all these years. Now it's yours."

I've never seen Dad's sentimental side before. Guess he'd been hiding it like I'd been hiding my Spark.

"It's the best, Dad." I give him a big hug. "And you're the best."

Mom wipes a tear from her eye, but then snaps her head

around and sniffs the air.

"Oh, I'd better get dinner out of the oven before it burns. Don't worry, sweetie. It's not pot roast."

Mom dashes out the door. Dad goes to follow her and turns back to me.

"Congratulations, Remmy!" We trade big grins. "Giocomo and Nonna would be so proud."

Then he follows Mom downstairs.

The music box stops and I wind the crank to hear the song again.

I take my Beatles concert ticket stub off the WOW!WALL. I place it and the brush inside the box. Laying on the red velvet, the stub and brush look like they're in a museum exhibit. Well, they *are* that valuable to me and my biggest treasures of the year. I add a guitar pick Bill gave me and a postcard of a Georgia O'Keeffe painting from Mrs. Egan.

When the New Year started by cracking open the treasure chest of 1965, I couldn't have predicted a year like this with its rocking ups and rolling downs. Sticking to my resolution wasn't easy, but I did it. My Spark of an Artist shines bright.

And it's only the end of August. Wonder what the rest of the year will bring?

Author's Note:

My Life in the 1960s

The *Art of Being Remmy* was inspired by the most exciting event in my young life—at the age of 13, I was a winner in a WABC Radio Draw The Beatles art contest. With the other winners, I received Beatles concert tickets from disc jockey Big Dan Ingram at the New York Worlds Fair. Then, on August 29, 1964, my best friend Dana (who was in NO way like Debbie) and I screamed our way through the Beatles singing at the Forest Hills Tennis Stadium in Queens, New York.

I was born to be an artist. But unlike Remmy's father, my parents fully supported my talents and I started oil painting lessons at age 9 with a neighborhood mom. My art classes through middle school and high school introduced me to pen and ink, watercolor, printmaking, sculpture, even jewelry making. I'm fortunate I grew up in a town that was committed to the arts.

Historical note: Like Remmy, I naively thought I would meet the Beatles at the concert, since I was a big winner. But no such luck. 28 years later, however, I was on a painting vacation in England and I bumped into PAUL MCCARTNEY on a street and shook his hand. See? Dreams can come true.

Me and my award-winning cartoon (left). Dana and I at the NY World's Fair (above).

Getting my tickets from "Big Dan" (above). The Beatles in concert (below)—snapped with my Kodak Brownie Starmite (left).

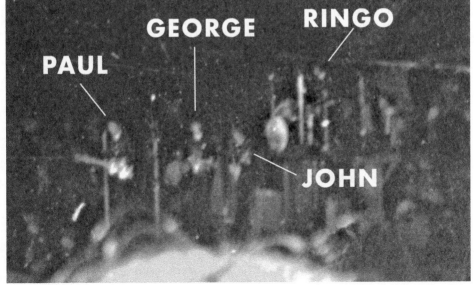

PAUL

GEORGE

RINGO

JOHN

The Modern Women's Movement: 1960s–1980s

Remmy felt that something wasn't fair to girls in the mid-sixties and I had the same feelings back then. I loved to play baseball, but there were no teams for girls. Boys learned to use tools in shop class while girls sewed and cooked in home economics class. Boys wore pants. Girls wore dresses and skirts. There seemed to be an unwritten code that girls and boys had different rules to live by.

A rumbling of discontent began in the hearts of some women. There was "a problem with no name" as Betty Friedan wrote in her 1963 book, *The Feminine Mystique*.

When it was time for me to go to college in the late 1960s, my commercial artist uncle advised that I study to be an art teacher. He felt that it was a good job for a girl because I could teach until I got married and had children. Then I would be able to go back to teaching when my kids were old enough.

So that was the plan. But, as it turned out, once I got to college, I discovered graphic design—a great career and better fit for me.

By the time I got graduated college (the same year that the first issue of *Ms.* magazine was published in 1972), the rumbling from the early sixties had turned into a full-blown women's movement that tackled issues of gender inequality and brought about historic events for American women:

1966: **The National Organization for Women (NOW)** is founded to promote equal rights for women.

1967: **Kathy Switzer** becomes the first woman to register and run the Boston Marathon (even though organizers along the route attempted to physically pull her out of the race).

1968: **Shirley Chisholm** becomes the first African-American woman elected to Congress (representing Brooklyn, N.Y.).

1972: **Title IX (Public Law 92-318) of the Education Amendments** prohibits sex discrimination in all aspects of education programs that receive federal support. This greatly increased opportunities for girls in sports.

1974: After lawsuits, **Little League Baseball's** ban of girls is lifted. Little League Softball is also created.

1981: **Sandra Day O'Connor** becomes the first female U.S. Supreme Court judge.

1983: Astronaut **Sally Ride** blasts off as the first American woman in space.

1987: **The National Museum of Women in the Arts** opens in Washington, D.C.

1987: H.W. Janson's *History of Art* FINALLY includes women in the book. Remmy would be pleased. But still, only 27 women (out of 318 artists) are represented in the most current 9th edition of H.W. Janson's survey, *Basic History of Western Art.*

Generations of women have opened doors for women of the next generation. Keep opening doors for yourself and all who come after you.

Art Appendix
Did you find all these artists' names in this novel?

MICHELANGELO BUONARROTI (1475 –1564) was an Italian sculptor, painter, and architect of the High Renaissance. He's well known for his sculptures, the *Pietà* and *David*, and for his frescos on the ceiling and altar wall of the Sistine Chapel in Rome.

MARY CASSATT (1844 –1926) was born in Pennsylvania, but moved to Paris to study art. She exhibited with the Impressionists, and is know for images of women and the bond between mothers and children.

PAUL CÉZANNE (1839 – 1906) was a French Post-Impressionist painter. His portraits, still lifes, and landscapes were painted in planes of color and small brushstrokes.

EL GRECO (1541 – 1614) was a painter, sculptor, and architect of the Spanish Renaissance known for his religious paintings with elongated, dramatic figures.

PAUL GAUGUIN (1848 – 1903) was a French Post-Impressionist artist. Towards the end of his life, he moved to Tahiti, painting the people and landscapes from that tropical region.

JON GNAGY (1907 – 1981) was a self-taught artist most remembered for being America's original television art instructor, hosting his syndicated *Learn to Draw* series. His very helpful art kits are still available for sale.

HANS HOLBEIN THE YOUNGER (1497 – 1543) was a German artist who worked in a Northern Renaissance style. He's known for his portraits of the aristocracy in 16th-century England.

LEE KRASNER (1908 – 1984) was an accomplished American Abstract Expressionist painter, although overshadowed by her husband, painter Jackson Pollack.

LEONARDO DA VINCI (1452 – 1519) was an Italian painter, sculptor, architect, and inventor— a true "Renaissance man." The *Mona Lisa* is his most famous painting.

JOAN MIRÓ (1893 – 1983) was a Spanish Surrealist painter, sculptor, and ceramicist born in Barcelona.

AMEDEO MODIGLIANI (1884 – 1920) was an Italian painter and sculptor who worked in France. His portraits were painted in a style characterized by elongation of faces and figures.

PIET MONDRIAN (1872 – 1944) was a Dutch painter and a pioneer of 20th century abstract art, painting compositions of simple geometric elements.

(Top) *The Starry Night* by Vincent van Gogh.
(Bottom, l-r) *Self-portrait Leaning on a Sill* by Rembrandt van Rijn,
The Letter by Mary Cassatt, and *Portrait of Henry VIII* by Hans Holbein.

Images: National Gallery of Art, WikiMedia, Google Arts & Culture

CLAUDE MONET (1840 – 1926) was a founder of French Impressionist painting, and is known for his landscapes and studies of the water lilies in his Giverny gardens.

GIORGIO MORANDI (1890 – 1964) was an Italian painter and printmaker who specialized in still life. His paintings were limited mainly to vases, bottles, bowls, flowers and landscapes focusing on subtle gradations of hue and tone.

GRANDMA MOSES (Anna Mary Robertson Moses) (1860 – 1961) was an American folk artist. She began painting at the age of 78 and is known for charming country scenes of rural New England.

ALICE NEEL (1900 – 1984) was an American painter of bold, expressive portraits of art-world celebrities and neighbors in Spanish Harlem, New York City.

GEORGIA O'KEEFFE (1887 – 1986) was a pioneer of American Modernism known for her paintings of enlarged flowers, New York skyscrapers, and New Mexico landscapes.

PABLO PICASSO (1881 – 1973) was a Spanish painter, sculptor, printmaker, and ceramicist. He spent most of his adult life in France and was one of the most influential artists of the 20th century, known for co-founding the Cubist movement, and the co-invention of collage.

PETER PAUL RUBENS (1577 – 1640) was a Flemish Baroque painter of portraits, and scenes of mythology and allegory. He was fond of painting full-figured women, giving rise to the term 'Rubenesque'.

NORMAN ROCKWELL (1894 – 1978) was a 20th-century American painter and illustrator. He is most famous for magazine cover illustrations of everyday American life.

VINCENT VAN GOGH (1853 – 1890) was a Dutch Post-Impressionist painter and one of the most famous and influential figures in the history of Western art. Created mostly in France, his still lifes, portraits, and self-portraits vibrate with bold colors and expressive brushwork.

REMBRANDT VAN RIJN (1606 – 1669) was a Dutch painter, and printmaker. His paintings and etchings range from portraits and self-portraits to landscapes, and allegorical and historical scenes.

JAMES ABBOTT MCNEILL WHISTLER (1834 – 1903) was an artist during the American Gilded Age and based primarily in the United Kingdom. His most famous painting is *Arrangement in Grey and Black No. 1* (1871), commonly known as *Whistler's Mother*.

Acknowledgements

Remmy and I have been on a long journey together and had lots of help along the way.

Thanks to the New Jersey chapter of SCBWI (Society of Children's Book Writers and Illustrators) for providing many years of conferences, workshops, retreats, and critiques from editors, agents, and authors. I've learned so much and truly found my tribe in the friends I've made through SCBWI.

I'm grateful for the magic that is the Highlights Foundation. Tucked in the Pocono mountains, the Foundation gave me my own cabin and the chance to work with mentors Alan Gratz, Patti Lee Gauch, and Kathryn Erskine. Again, I found advice and friendship from other mentees.

Thank you to my critique buddies through the years: The Tale Spinners (Nona, Alexis, Suzanne, Elisabeth, Helen, and Kim), and writer friends who helped in the beginning, Connie, Darlene, and Kami.

Special love to my parents, Mary and Tony Zisk, who were so supportive of all my dreams, and for sitting patiently on a bench outside the Beatles concert while my dear friend Dana and I screamed our hearts out inside.

And a big smooch to my daughter, Anna, for understanding when I was in the zone, for tolerating a messy house, and for pushing me to not give up. I love you.

About The Author

Mary Zisk is a graphic designer (mostly of magazines) and an artist with a passion for capturing foreign destinations in watercolor. She is the author and illustrator of the picture book, *The Best Single Mom in the World: How I Was Adopted*. She blogs about her many eclectic collections at TheClutterChronicles.com. Mary lives in New Jersey with her daughter and four white fluffy rescue mutts.

MARY ZISK
Creative, bowling,
Art Staff, dogs,
Oil Painting Club

The Art of Being Remmy is her debut middle grade novel.

For more information, visit **www.MaryZisk.com**.

CPSIA information can be obtained
at www.ICGtesting.com
Printed in the USA
LVHW090006080519
617045LV00004B/38/P